The stone gripped him like a vise. Its hold was punishing, gripping his shoulders, compressing his chest and back. Too late he recalled the warning that the passageway narrowed drastically here. He had rammed himself right into it; now, like a cork stoppering a flask of wine, he was held.

Panic ripped through him, but now his old pride and will to fight rose up as well. If he was to die, even in this wretched place, in this manner, he would die as befit a war prince of the Arcturian Empire . . .

Ace books by P. M. Griffin

STAR COMMANDOS
STAR COMMANDOS: COLONY IN PERIL
STAR COMMANDOS: MISSION UNDERGROUND

STAR COMMANDOS

MISSION UNDER GROUND

P.M. GRIFFIN

ACE BOOKS, NEW YORK

This book is an Ace original edition,
and has never been previously published.

STAR COMMANDOS:
MISSION UNDERGROUND

An Ace Book/published by arrangement with
the author

PRINTING HISTORY
Ace edition / October 1988

ISBN: 0-441-77938-7

Ace Books are published by
The Berkley Publishing Group,
200 Madison Avenue, New York, New York 10016.
The name "ACE" and the "A" logo are trademarks
belonging to Charter Communications, Inc.
PRINTED IN THE UNITED STATES OF AMERICA

10 9 8 7 6 5 4 3 2 1

To my father, Timothy Griffin,
ever a companion and advisor
in adventure.

ONE

RAM SITHE LOOKED up from his desk as Commando-Colonel Islaen Connor came into the office. He returned her salute and then waved her into the chair before him.

"Sit, Colonel. I have a job for you."

The woman merely nodded slightly as she took her seat. She had guessed as much when she had received this summons. Admiral Sithe would know full well that the latest round of work on the *Fairest Maid* was nearly completed and the starship could be readied for space in short order.

"Aye, sir?"

"It's not really your kind of work, and normally I wouldn't consider sending you at all, but there is some need for speed on us, and your *Maid*'s fast."

"Besides, whatever the problem is, you'd feel better for having a Commando handle it?"

"I would," the Admiral replied. "What do you know about Hades of Persephone?"

She thought for a few moments. "Nothing."

"That's hardly surprising. She's never played a very significant role—just another backwater world, like so many others.

"Her recent history has been unfortunate. The Arcturians took her during the second year of the War, but their plans to use her as a jump-off for deeper penetration altered almost as soon as they had secured her. The main conflict turned suddenly and had moved out of her part of space entirely within a few months. The invasion fleet garrisoning her never made the sweep for which it was originally intended, nor was it

1

withdrawn, since there was reason to fear the possibility of a Federation counterattack through that region, an assault that never came.''

"So they just stagnated there for all those years?'' Islaen asked grimly; she could imagine what that had meant for the local populace.

"Precisely. The fleet involved was a relatively small one, but still, the Empire was rarely guilty of being so wasteful in the deployment of its manpower. It was a surprising lapse, especially in the face of the pressure we were putting on them near the end.

"Anyway, Hades had supported a small Navy base and a major arsenal before the invasion. Fortunately, word of the coming attack did reach the military. —It was the first intelligence coup we had, and the only one for some time. —The planet could not be defended with the forces at hand, and there was no hope of summoning aid, not with our ships fleeing before the Emperor's armadas on every side, so the commander chose to evacuate his people to preserve them as a fighting force. He recognized the responsibility the arsenal put on him as well and brought away all the classified matériel and as much of the other major weapons as he could. The remainder—and it was a vast store—was turned over to the planetary leaders for use by the already forming Resistance.

"Each cell, as they called their units, got a share, which was promptly hidden in the caverns honeycombing all Hades' crust, in locations known only to the members of each individual group. With these stores they were able to wreak terrible havoc on their invaders.''

The Admiral's normally impassive face tightened visibly.

"The Hadesim are a harsh, violent folk capable of conceiving fierce hatreds and strong enough to carry them to their consummation, whatever the consequences to themselves. They fought constantly and bitterly, and because they went into the War so well-armed against an enemy virtually marooned and forgotten themselves, they succeeded to an astonishing degree. By the War's end they had destroyed most of the Arcturian ships and had set their badly decimated oppressors completely on the defensive. So far did they gain their ends that it took the arrival of our fleet to enforce the cease-fire.

They wanted no ending of the hostilities while a single Arcturian soldier remained alive.''

"That kind of hate is usually merited," the Commando said quietly.

"It was. They had suffered horribly. Hades wasn't another Thorne. Orlan Fran Uskorn and his son, who assumed command upon his retirement, were both proper savages. They utterly lacked Varn Tarl Sogan's ability to think unconventionally, like a guerrilla, and they felt nothing but contempt for the menials-turned-warriors who were their opponents. The population had shrunk to less than a fifth of its preinvasion level by the time of the surrender.''

The woman's eyes closed. Thorne had indeed been fortunate. "It's a wonder one or the other of them didn't order a burn-off," she said.

"They both realized it would be an admission of total defeat, I suppose—the open declaration before the Empire, and the Federation as well, that they were incapable of securing their command. That's the reason Captain Sogan has given for why relatively few commanders issued that order, despite heavy Resistance pressure. It's probably the only thing that saved Hades. Both Uskorns were more than capable of slaughtering a planet.''

"How does all this involve us now?" Islaen Connor asked.

"Most of the remaining weapons were returned to the Navy at the War's close, all save those in one cache. The location of that one wasn't known, since all of the cell controlling it were believed dead, victims of an accidental detonation of their own explosives in the final days of active warfare.

"Two weeks ago a survivor surfaced and came to Patrol headquarters on Hades. He volunteered to take us to it.''

"Why now?"

"Because he had just discovered that another comrade also remains alive and may possibly be dealing with pirates.'' His eyes locked with hers. "There's a planetbuster in that cache, Colonel. The Hadesim don't want to be even indirectly responsible for what it could do if it falls into the hands of that space scum, and neither do we. We have to get it back.''

She nodded, but frowned as well. "Why send me, sir? It seems like straight diplomat's work.''

"Technically it is, but as I told you, the weapons were stored underground. The rest of them have been returned already, but no one will touch that missile. You see, it can't come out as it is. It must be dismantled first, and if it goes off in that confined space, it will most assuredly live up to its name as far as Karst, the planet's capital, is concerned. The city's sitting smack on top of it."

She stared at him. "Commandos know a good bit about explosives, sir, but I can't handle that thing."

"I don't expect you to handle it," the Admiral told her impatiently. "Fortune's with us in one respect. The best damn demolitions expert we had in all the Navy is now working aboard a freighter servicing Jade of Kuan Yin. We've contacted her, and your friend Jake Karmikel is flying her to Hades as fast as his *Jovian Moon* can bring her. If you lift now, you would both reach there at about the same time."

"What exactly is to be my role?"

"To officiate, to represent the Federation. It's because pirates may be involved, and because it will be necessary to function in strange and maybe very rugged terrain, that I want a Commando in charge."

He frowned. "Unfortunately, there could be difficulties apart from the outside possibility of treachery. The locals bear no love for the Federation military, since we gave them no help during their long ordeal."

Sithe paused and seemed to study her closely for a few moments, until she began to feel uncomfortable under his gaze.

"They also hate anything that resembles an Arcturian, to the point that they've removed off-world everyone taller than the norm for their race, or anyone bearing dark hair or eyes, even some of their very young children."

"The invaders' get?"

He shook his head. "Those were slain at birth, and their mothers with them if there was so much as the shadow of a suspicion that there might have been any degree of consent. . . . As I said before, this is a hard people."

His black eyes caught and held hers once more. "Captain Sogan will do well to planet with you and lift again without allowing himself to be seen. If he's had trouble on a world like Horus, he is certain to find it on that wretched hole."

"Are you suggesting that I would do well to find some other transport to Hades?" she asked evenly.

"No. You need the *Maid*'s speed, and even if you didn't, I don't presume to tell my Commando officers how to run their missions once they have an assignment. I'm just warning you of a potential complication."

The woman lowered her head but raised it again a moment later. "A warning I appreciate and shall heed, sir. Thank you." Her eyes narrowed.

"Whatever a team's care, accidents can happen, especially when pirates or the subbiotics who deal with them are involved. What if we wind up disarming that weapon only to have it taken from us?"

Ram Sithe smiled coldly. "You have three weeks. If we hear nothing from you in that time, the Navy goes in. No wolf pack's picking up a tool with which to terrorize half the Sector. In the meantime Hades of Persephone is completely blockaded. Nothing but the *Fairest Maid* and the *Jovian Moon* is getting on or off her, and those only with proper identification."

He rose to his feet. "I guess that's about it, Colonel. How soon do you think you can lift?"

"Probably by this afternoon, sir. Maybe in a couple of hours, if Varn has finished checking her out. Once he's done with that, we need only fuel her up and bring in our supplies."

"Good enough. Let me hear from you once the planetbuster has been secured." He sighed. "You *should* be able to get to it and bring it off-world without any trouble. I hope it works out that way."

TWO

Islaen Connor secured her flier beside the beautifully proportioned needle-nose which was now her home as well as her transport through the far-flung reaches of the mighty Federation ultrasystem.

She darted up the boarding ramp and disengaged the seals on the hatch. Only the ship locks were set. That meant Varn was on board. Had he left the *Maid* for any reason, he would have secured the others as well.

The woman's eyes shadowed for a moment. Such preoccupation with security was not the norm among spacers, but then, her husband—or consort, as he would have said—had reason to be cautious. The memories and hatreds of the recent War were still sharp, and the scars it had left were deep. No Arcturian would dare to move openly on any Federation planet, much less here on the rim, where discovery in many areas would mean a quick but brutal death.

Anger flashed through her. That was to her kind's disgrace. The Federation had known many heroes since the exploration of the stars had begun, but few of them had acted more valiantly or more humanely at such cost than Varn Tarl Sogan, and he had done so not once, but several times over.

Islaen compelled herself to relax as she passed through the hatch, lest he pick up her mood. She did not want him to realize she worried as much as she did about him.

Once inside, her mind sought his. A moment later the Commando smiled as their thoughts touched and she received his greeting. There was no mistaking the pleasure in his welcome, and the happiness in it lightened her own mood.

She was hardly surprised to find that the former Admiral was still in the drive room. The Navy technicians had just finished their latest series of innovations on *Fairest Maid* that morning, and he would want to study their work, trace and retrace what they had done until it all but became part of his own mind.

That intimacy with his ship was no quirk, no crutch adopted by a lonely and memory-haunted man, but a necessity for anyone who would captain a ship along the starlanes and beyond. Those who failed to achieve it usually did not travel far before dying, and many of them died very cruelly.

Her chin raised. No fear of that with this one. Space was Sogan's element, and few, if any, could equal him there. All too many Federation officers had learned that to their dismay before his fleet had been removed from the kind of combat which had won him his fame and assigned to invade and hold Thorne of Brandine during the final years of the War.

She drew her thoughts back from the events of the past. Now was not the time to be wandering there, not with present and future work to be done.

Varn, her thought asked, *how long before we can lift? We have a mission.*

So soon? he responded in mild surprise.

Aye. It's nothing much. I'll tell you about it later, but Admiral Sithe would like us to get a move on.

Give me a couple of hours. We can go sooner, but there are a few of these circuits that I do not entirely trust.

Take all the time you need. We won't accomplish anything if we blow ourselves to space dust. —I'll change now, and then go to the crew's cabin. Join me when you get a minute. You can probably use a break, and we can go over our latest job there.

Will do, Colonel.

He severed the contact with that, and Islaen chuckled. He was probably glad to get back to his precious maze of wires and chips.

She caught hold of the core ladder, which ran the length of the *Maid*, giving access to every part of her. Scaling it with the ease of long custom, she soon swung herself off on the deck supporting Sogan's quarters and her own.

She entered her cabin, unfastened the snaps closing her

high, tight collar, and made a wry face at herself. Varn seemed to find no discomfort in a dress uniform, but then, he had almost literally been bred to wear the things. She had never even thought to adopt one of any sort until the War and the pressure it had put on her family had moved her to enlist. After that, well, guerrillas, by the very nature of their work, more often fought in disguise than in strict military garb.

Islaen pulled off the stark black tunic but paused a moment before reaching for a more comfortable one to replace it. As always when her eyes fell on it, she was held by the utter beauty of the gem gleaming against her white skin.

It was big, slightly better than thirty karats in weight, and of a marvelous clarity and brilliance. In color, it was a vivid blue-green, and it was formed like a drop of water frozen by some incomprehensible magic as it fell. Within this, as its very heart, was another, tiny drop, equally perfect and of a deeper shade of the same fine color.

A river tear. Only three planets in all the ultrasystem were known to have produced them, two old sources and now Jade of Kuan Yin, and her possession of them must remain a secret. Only her own settlers and a handful of others, all sworn to silence, were aware of the deposits. Some day they would be the planet's wealth, but for now they must be kept hidden until the new colony was well enough established to exploit and guard them. Otherwise they would be no benefit, but a grave danger.

Her large brown eyes glittered coldly. That had been made all too clear by the betrayal of the settlers by their own Settlement Agent, a betrayal that would have annihilated the colony had she and Sogan not accidentally discovered the plot and thwarted it.

That was the second time they had saved those people, and for that reason—and because of the trust and the real love the Amonites felt for the two off-worlders—the Amonites had given them the jewel, knowing their trust was soundly placed.

Her expression softened. The colonists had learned from their gurries, those tiny, mind-reading marvels native to Jade, how very deeply the former Admiral longed to have one of the stones, and they had so adroitly pressed this on him that he had not been able to refuse.

Sogan, in turn, had given it to her, as he had been aching

to do since he had first seen Jade's treasure. His inability to do so had been both a shame and a torment to him, for it violated the custom of his people, his own natural generosity, and his love for her. Realizing that, she had been unable to refuse it, to refuse him.

Islaen pulled on the pale green tunic she had selected and carefully settled the river tear so it rode easily on her breast. She wore it openly when they were alone.

A whistling call sounding simultaneously in her ears and mind broke into her thoughts. She hastily opened the door and raised her left hand, palm up, fingers slightly curled to receive the tiny winged creature that streaked into the cabin.

It was brown, with a black stripe circling the head and eyes like a mask. Those eyes were black as well, bright and incredibly merry. The bill beneath them was flexible enough to display a variety of expressions. It was a cheerful yellow, as were the feet and the supple toes, each crowned with a sharp claw, now properly sheathed. Although feathered and airborne, the newcomer was a mammal, not a member of one of the vast avian class.

"Hello, love," the woman said as her fingers curled around the gurry.

She and Varn nearly always used verbal speech with the gurry when they were alone, although Bandit could receive their thoughts as readily as she transmitted her own. It was no conscious choice on their part, and Islaen Connor was not even really aware that she had reverted to it as she spoke her greeting. When they were with anyone besides Jake or, now that they had gurries of their own, Jade's settlers, she automatically used mind touch, for the fact that the little creatures could communicate with humans in this fashion—and influence their feelings—was a greater secret even than the presence of river tears on their planet. It was a precaution needed to protect Jade's denizens, human and nonhuman alike, from the invasion of scientists and other officials who would descend if news of this relationship were ever to reach them; no one appreciated that fact more than the two off-worlders who had initially become aware of it on the morning when Bandit had adopted her.

That event had marked the beginning of a new and more exciting life plan for the settlers who had come to Jade of

Kuan Yin thinking only to manage stock, and it had added a great deal of joy and pleasure to her life and to Varn Tarl Sogan's.

She caressed the Jadite creature even more tenderly. "Well, did you get tired of watching Varn play with his circuits?"

Bandit doesn't like engines. Too dirty, and they smell. The gurry's oddly supple bill wrinkled as she broadcast that thought. *Besides, Varn forgets me when he's with them.*

"What a tragic fate for a gurry!" The Commando chuckled. She stroked the upturned head and neck with her forefinger. "Never mind, love. I have something here that I think will please you."

An ear-splitting whistle of pure delight answered her as she drew a packet from one of the pouches on her belt and opened it. The gurry liked native Horus sweetnuts almost as much as the considerably more costly Terran chocolate. The woman gave her a piece.

"I've laid in a store of all sorts of good things so you won't feel deprived when we lift again.—Go easy, will you? There are limits as to how big a gurry should grow!"

Nooo! Bandit will take only enough! she replied after hurriedly pecking up the final crumb.

"I wonder."

Islaen wouldn't give too much, she answered serenely.

Now the Colonel smiled. "That's pure trickery, my feathered friend. You're trying to manage me, and as usual, it works, coming from you."

She straightened. "Let's go. I told Varn that I'd see him in the crew's cabin. We do have a mission, such as it is, and I don't want to keep him waiting."

The cabin designed for use by the *Maid*'s crew and by any rare passengers when no duties occupied them was small, as were all the starship's compartments, but it was pleasantly and efficiently appointed.

The color scheme was a restful blue and gray, easy on the eyes and the nerves alike. The furniture was simple and multifunctional, all of it securely fastened to prevent damage or injury during an emergency. It followed the usual pattern and consisted chiefly of padded, high-backed benches set along the walls, with a table between them at the blind end where three of the walls met. Two doors led from the cabin, one to the core ladder, the other to the minute mess and the galley branching off from it.

Stored in the drawers, files, and cabinets built beneath the benches were the books, tapes, and other materials and equipment that made the hours between planetfalls full and profitable ones.

The master of the *Fairest Maid* had not yet arrived, and Islaen used the time given her by his absence to store some of the supplies she had brought back with her, including several new tapes.

She sighed as she slid the last into its place. Only two had been bought purely for their delight. She had requisitioned the rest, which contained information that might prove useful to them on Hades of Persephone. Even on a straightforward run like this, she could not forget her war-honed instinct to anticipate the worst and try to provide against it.

Ah well, she thought, she had never worked beneath a planet's crust before. It could do her no harm to learn a bit about the world's history and people, about what she might expect to encounter there and how she might have to function in that strange, perpetually dark realm.

Her mood lightened again as she felt another approaching, and she looked up as Varn Tarl Sogan came into the cabin.

He was a moderately tall, slender man with the dark brown hair and eyes and the olive skin of his race, as well as the strong, hard features marking the position into which he had been born within it. Those features could mean his death, were the significance of them to be recognized in the wrong company.

There was nothing whatsoever remarkable in his clothing. That was merely the garb typical of any spacer, much stained with lubricant now, after his many hours of exploration in the drive room. His stance, too, did not set him terribly apart. It was that of a soldier, which was hardly remarkable after the general demobilization of the Navy following the close of the war. The ultrasystem was full of former warriors.

It was apparent to anyone at all capable of reading men that he had once held rank of some importance. The custom of command rested on him like a cloak, that and the quiet assurance of one long used to having the fate of others ride upon his decisions.

There was an aloofness about him, as well, which kept most people at a distance; that and a cold strength of will which those who worked the outer rim recognized as a signal of potential danger.

Sogan knew full well the effect he had upon others, and either shrugged it off or actively played upon it, depending on the situation. He wanted no contact with most of the Federation's peoples, and had good reason to fear it in a great many instances.

Islaen Connor did not blame him for that. Why should he trust or want to trust half a galaxy of strangers, of enemies? His own race had used him brutally, broken him in rank and in body in one of the greatest miscarriages of justice born of the bitterness engendered by the War. Strong minds had shattered under far less than he had endured. It was a miracle that his had not, and it was a powerful testament to the man he was that he had not turned entirely to bitterness and hate himself.

All this swept through her mind in that first instant of sighting him and vanished again as her whole being brightened under the surge of happiness with which he always welcomed her, a joy and open warmth in total contrast to the reserve that was his mask and marked his dealings with the rest of their species. She gloried in the splendor of it even as she wondered how she had come to mean so much to him.

The former Admiral's greeting was casual, as befitted their brief separation, merely a smile and a slight lifting of his hand.

He seated himself on the edge of the table and reached over to rub Bandit.

"So there you are, little one. Did you get tired of being ignored, and come in search of more congenial company?"

The hen, who was in her favorite perch on Islaen's shoulder, raised her head to receive his caress.

Yes.

The woman smiled and linked her mind with his. *Never give a gurry an opening like that, friend. It can be hard on the ego.*

So I observe. His eyes went to the jewel glinting on her

breast. "It looks good," he remarked after the briefest of pauses.

His use of audible speech surprised her. They rarely resorted to it when alone. A gentle probe revealed that his shields were up as well. Something was bothering him again, then.

Islaen, accustomed to responding to his moods, only nodded. She answered him in kind. "That it does. I'm glad I was able to get it set without arousing any suspicions."

"Everyone on Horus knows we have credits to spend, with a brace of heroism citations each and a third split between us." He fell silent again, as if groping for words.

"I have been thinking about those credits. Your Navy is doing all the work on the *Maid*, and even after setting a good sum aside for emergencies, we still have a respectable amount left over."

"You have some way in mind for disposing of a bit of it?" she asked curiously, thoroughly surprised by the drift of the conversation.

He looked away from her. "We are still entitled to a furlough, since our stay on Jade turned out to be anything but that. You have mentioned how much you enjoyed your brief visit to Hedon. Why not take our leave when we finish with this latest mission you mention, and go there for a while?"

The woman stared at him. "Hedon? Have you been sipping opaline?—You're uncomfortable here on Horus where you know you've got the support of the whole military command, and you're not even entirely happy on Jade. What in all space is moving you to suggest planeting on a mobbed inner-system world, especially that one?"

"She has much to offer," he replied defensively. "I cannot allow reasonable caution to grow into paranoia. Besides, a pleasure planet boasts luxury goods, and Hedon's jewel merchants are reputed to have the finest stocks in the Federation. We could pick you up one or two companions for your river tear if we looked carefully."

Islaen quelled her surge of anger that Sogan was reverting to the past and treating her like a plaything, a living doll in a war prince's harem. She was wronging him there. He was afraid that his dread of exposure was imprisoning her here on the rim, depriving her of access to the richness and wonder of her ultrasystem; and he was willing to sacrifice his own need for isolation, and the security it brought, to amend that fancied wrong.

Why hadn't he told her this was gnawing at him? She could have put it to rest fast enough.

Once again Islaen willed her temper to cool. That was Varn. She had accepted it when she had accepted the man.

Suddenly all the love she had for him welled up within her. On this occasion, as on every other she had thus far encountered, it had been his concern and consideration for her that had moved him, never any worry of his own.

Her mind reached out to him, gently calling at his shields for admittance, and he opened himself to receive her.

He had not expected the rush of warmth that she brought with her, and Islaen Connor laughed softly at his astonishment.

Can't a woman show that she loves her husband?

Her thoughts grew more serious. The Arcturian would be most uncomfortable if he realized she had read him this closely. Part of his argument had, in fact, been sound reasoning, and she decided to use that to support his mask.

You're right about the stone. A couple of others of the right kind would draw some attention away from it, and Hedon would be the place to go for rarities that would still fit our purse. That'll have to wait for a bit, though. As you point out, we have a job to do first.

Aye. Your Admiral Sithe did not give us much time to recover from our battles on and over Jade.

This sort of just came up. It's hardly anything to excite us after our last few adventures, merely a matter of witnessing the return of some surplus Navy armaments.

She glanced in the direction of the galley. *Since you're more or less on your feet, how about getting us some jakek? We might as well relax while going over the details.*

THREE

SOGAN SWALLOWED A mouthful of the hot liquid, savoring its rich, smooth flavor, before setting his cup down and turning to his companion.

Now, Colonel, what about our mission? Where are we going?

To Hades of Persephone.

He frowned. *That hole?*

Islaen's brows arched. *You know her? That's more than I could claim when Admiral Sithe mentioned her to me.*

Sogan nodded. *Aye, or of her, rather. She was one of the first planets we seized at the War's beginning. At that time her role was to have been an important one, no less than the jump-off for a two-prong assault designed to divide the Federation into three parts. But circumstances dictated a change in our plans, and she became and remained an unpleasant eddy on the war maps.*

I argued against keeping a fleet penned there almost from the time I made Admiral. It was serving no useful purpose on Hades, and the threat of an invasion or attack from that Sector was not sufficient in my judgment to warrant holding those ships inactive when they could have been put to excellent use elsewhere.

His tone grew bleak. *Unfortunately, the surplanetary Resistance was very active and our Ruling Command would not permit a withdrawal lest it be imagined that we had been driven off.* He grimaced. *That folly at a time when we were starting to be forced off planets, important ones, for a fact!*

Sogan shrugged. *Six years before the War's end I was*

assigned to take and hold Thorne in preparation for a massive push against the Sectors of that region, and I had too many troubles of my own after that to worry about Hades. Or much else for that matter. . . . —That is past. What about now?

Islaen responded by describing her interview with Ram Sithe, fleshing out what he had told her with some of the information she had gleaned from the tape she had reviewed during her drive back to the starship.

You're right about an active Resistance. Lack of interstellar importance in no way lessened the fury of the on-world fighting.

Hades of Persephone is a harsh planet. Her people live chiefly by mining and exporting the heavy minerals she contains in reasonable abundance. They must delve for water as well, since only a comparatively small portion of her considerable supply exists on the surface. She has bred a hard race, and they fought the invaders with everything their cruel world, and fortune's one kind stroke in arming them well, gave them. They conducted their movement so successfully that even with occasional resupplying, the fleet could be maintained at no better than half strength in the War's later years.

He looked sharply at her. *Half an invasion fleet, more than that numerically, died on Hades?*

They were avenged. The local population count is now less than a fifth of its former total.

Varn was silent for several seconds. Thorne had fought viciously and with terrible singleness of purpose to regain her freedom, but her battle had not called down destruction of this magnitude, not on her own people or on the soldiers of his fleet. What had happened on Hades of Persephone could only be termed a disaster, for the Empire and the Federation alike, all the more tragic because there had been so little real purpose in the invaders' presence there.

He drew his mind away from that grim, all-too-recent past. *Now we are to pick up matériel from one of the Resistance's ammunition dumps?*

"*Just one weapon. The rest have already been restored, but the planetbuster. . . .*

The former Admiral stiffened. *What were guerrillas doing with a major weapon like that?*

They were fighting a major war! Islaen glared at him as much in surprise as in annoyance. Varn had never spoken disparagingly of Resistance forces before. With his history on Thorne, he was hardly in a position to do so.

Neither had he on this occasion. Sogan quickly raised his hands, palms out, in the old gesture for peace.

Sorry, Colonel. I had not realized they were equipped to utilize such a thing.

No, I jumped you too fast. I'm in the wrong. —They weren't equipped to handle it, either, not as it was designed to be used, but as Admiral Sithe said, they're a harsh, somewhat violent, utterly unrelenting people, and they made the missile their ultimate weapon. Had their Resistance been broken completely, rather than accept the defeat and the slavery that would then come, they were prepared to detonate the planetbuster. Karst, their capital city, and all the surrounding countryside would've been totally annihilated, but the slaughter would have included most of their enemies, certainly all the ranking officers, and the better part of their equipment.

Islaen's fingers automatically soothed Bandit, whose feathers had ruffled in response to the chill that had rippled through both humans and radiated from them at her words.

Karst was lucky, and they weren't forced to use it.

So it still sits beneath the city, still armed and still deadly?

She nodded. *Navy technicians originally dismantled it so it could be brought through the narrow underground ways, and a Navy expert went with it—blindfolded so he wouldn't be able to reveal the depot's location should he fail to make his escape and be taken and questioned—in order to reassemble and arm it for them. Now none of the surplanetary leaders want to risk tampering with it, and they've demanded that the Navy do the work if we want the thing back.*

Varn eyed her carefully. *We do not have that kind of skill, not either of us.*

The Commando smiled, recalling her own initial reaction. *That's what I told Admiral Sithe, rather less calmly. We're not expected to tackle that particular part of the job, just witness that it's done and take the planetbuster away with us.*

Praise the Spirit of Space for that! he muttered. *Who, then?*

Jake's flying in. . . .

He frowned. *Karmikel?*

Aye. To our good fortune, one of the Federation's best demolitions people took a working berth on a freighter currently servicing Jade. The Navy traced her, and she's agreed to take this on. Jake's bringing her here on the Jovian Moon.

Sogan scarcely heard her, but he managed to throw off the dark thought pricking him before it could surface enough for his comrade to read.

What if your informant, this Larnse Greggs, is lying? he asked rather sharply, to turn the subject. *He claims humanitarian reasons drove him to contact the authorities, but what is the basis of his suspicions? Why would he turn on a former comrade in favor of those who gave no help in his world's War effort?*

Because of what a pirate raid entails, she replied. *Greggs only suspects the possibility of such contact, apparently, but he claims his associate was always an unscrupulous individual and is now a very bitter one, quite capable, at least in theory, of such intercourse. It's not a threat either his own planet's leaders or we can ignore.*

Hardly, as he well knows. Suppose Larnse Greggs is the unscrupulous one, the bitter one? His lips tightened. *Experiences such as Hades endured could drive a man mad. He might merely wish to draw officials or officers of the Navy, which did so little for his homeworld's underground, to some dark place where he could hope to work his will on them, even if there were no prospect of monetary gain at all.*

We'll have to accept that risk and depend on my skill to warn us against it. I've rarely failed to pick up a silent or dark thought from any human, particularly when it's directed against me or mine.

He nodded, satisfied. Her talent for detecting the emotions of those around her had served them well. He felt her eyes on him and met them. They seemed troubled, and he broke the contact again. Had she read him earlier?

Aye, Colonel?

Those people hate Arcturians, Varn.

No one in the Federation loves us, Colonel Connor.

Islaen started to speak again, but a low hissing sound caused both humans to glance at the gurry.

She had been following their conversation closely, and now the little hen's feathers were partially extended and her claws worked nervously, although without force, on the woman's shoulder.

Her bright eyes darted anxiously from one to the other of them. *Islaen, Varn, will we be having more trouble?*

"I don't know, love," the Commando replied. She reached up to curl her fingers closely around the creature, as if to shield her. "I hope with all I am that we don't, not with 300,000 people to pay for any mistakes we make."

FOUR

VARN TARL SOGAN smiled as he scanned the instrument panel on his bridge. The *Fairest Maid* was driving on at a speed he would once not have believed possible in a ship of any class, let alone one of this size, yet she moved without tremor, without any sign whatsoever of stress. The Navy's innovations and the work of its technicians were both faultless.

He settled back in his flight chair with a sigh of contentment and fixed his dark eyes on the universe beyond the narrow, transparent visual observation panels.

The splendor of that vast blackness held him now as it had always held him, the impossible glory of literally countless stars burning like fiery jewels in their ebony setting, seemingly minute sparks exquisite in their beauty and almost painful in their perfection.

The sight of them sent a fierce surge of longing and also a deep sense of peace flooding through him, and his eyes lowered for a moment.

Not very long ago there had been no peace in him. He remembered the three nightmare years following his exile, years without hope or purpose when these same distant sparks had shone forth as beacons calling him to the only ease or escape he could ever again expect to find in this mortal realm. So powerful had been the pull that several times he had been forced to use all the strength of his will to keep from setting course for one of those far galaxies, thereby severing himself from everything human for all the remainder of eternity.

He shuddered as the urgency of that inner demand returned for a moment. Was it compliance with the harsh will of the

Empire's gods that had kept him from obeying it, or a subtle form of defiance? Maybe something entirely different had held him back, a purely human stubbornness that refused to surrender completely, despite fate's crushing, irreparable blows.

Varn forcibly drew his thoughts back from the course they were following. It was still not a safe one, not even yet, though he had true life now, rather than hated existence, and the stars beyond were once more symbols of that life.

His reverie broke off abruptly. His consort was coming up, and there was some trouble on her.

When she reached the bridge, the Commando's expression confirmed his reading of her. She greeted him but did not say anything more for a moment, as if she were seeking a way to begin.

His eyes darkened, and he rose to meet her. *What has happened, Islaen?*

Nothing, she hastened to assure him, *but I've been going over the tapes on Hades that I brought with us. Varn, Admiral Sithe was right. When we planet, I want you to remain with the ship. I'll take care of whatever's to be done on-world.*

He looked at her sharply. *Is this some sort of jest?*

Unfortunately not. The Hadesim don't just hate your race. They hate anything that even vaguely resembles an Arcturian. Her eyes fixed his. *You won't have to be identified. Your appearance is enough to condemn you.*

Do you imagine I can let you go amongst such a people alone?

I'm very obviously no daughter of the Empire, she reminded him. *Besides, I won't be alone. Jake'll be with me.*

Varn scowled. "That is small comfort to me," he snapped, switching suddenly to verbal speech as he threw his mind shields into place.

"It'll have to suffice," Islaen replied.

Her answer came sharply. She had expected some protest from him, but this abrupt exclusion from his thoughts both surprised her and annoyed her considerably.

He shook his head. "I think not. I refuse to cower before dirt-clawing menials of this sort. I am an officer of the Federation Navy on Federation assignment. Let them swallow that."

Her eyes flashed. "I dislike your arrogance, Admiral! —You

might do well to remember that no fleets fly at your command now. You wear only a Captain's insignia here, and it's my order that carries the weight."

He stiffened as if he had taken the lash of a force whip in the face. "If this is your direct command, I shall, of course, obey it. Colonel."

Islaen gripped herself. He would comply. He was too much a soldier to do otherwise, but he was furious.

What had she just done? This was a difficulty they both had recognized might some day arise, although neither of them had ever spoken of it. They had always worked as a team, as equals, despite the disparity in their ranks, and the present situation did not justify her summarily bludgeoning his will. A frayed temper, not judgment, had driven her to speak as she had.

Well, she was still angry. Sogan had to realize she was right. She had never before known him to be unreasonable, and guessed that something must be tearing at him, but as long as he refused to trust her, he would have to fight it out by himself. She could not help him if he would not let her.

She glared at him. "Very well. I don't particularly want to see you slaughtered for no reason, or get killed myself trying to shield you, but as long as it's only your own life that you're risking and not our mission, I won't give any orders. Do whatever you want."

With that, she turned smartly on her heel and quit the bridge without looking at him or speaking to him again.

No sooner had the woman gone than Bandit rose to her full height on her perch on the copilot's seat, extending her feathers until she seemed to double in size. She faced Varn with an outraged hiss, but then the anger melted from her and she whimpered miserably.

Her patent distress cooled his temper, and he hastened over to her. Poor little thing! She had never experienced ill feeling between them before, and she was both bewildered and terrified by their exchange.

"Do not fear, small one," he told her, stroking her gently. "It would take more than this to sever us." His hand dropped to his side. "Go to Islaen now. She is upset and has need of you."

You're better. You come.

He shook his head. "Our tempers are still too hot for us to be together. —Go. I would be by myself for a while."

This time the gurry obeyed, although she flew slowly and looked back at him several times before finally moving out of his line of sight.

The Arcturian gave a sigh of relief when he found himself alone, and pressed his hands to his eyes, a gesture he had unconsciously taken from his consort. He felt weary, beaten. He had managed all this very poorly. Islaen had been entirely correct, and in his insistence upon having his own will, he had all but provoked that scene between them.

Sogan stopped himself. No. He was not so innocent. He had deliberately provoked it. He had known how she would respond to that remark about menials, to his whole manner, but the alternative had been even more unacceptable, more threatening. His stand would not have withstood logical assault. Since he was unwilling to abandon it and would never reveal the base fears firing it, he had chosen to drive this wedge between them.

His face tightened. He had in fact lied to her, in deed if not actually in word, and he chilled at the thought of the price such duplicity might eventually exact from him.

The former Admiral caught hold of himself. Panic would no more serve him now than in the midst of any other crisis. It had already drawn him to turn what should have been a minor difficulty into a very nasty situation.

Very well. He had discovered depths within himself that he did not like. It was his to come to terms with them, to do battle with them as he had battled every other challenge life had set before him.

His shoulders squared. This problem was his, and it was his to face and settle. His weakness, his failure to do so, had already caused enough pain. Now, before that injury could form into a crippling scar, he must do what he could to heal it.

Varn found the Colonel bent over a tape reader she had set up on the table in the crew's cabin. Bandit was sitting beside her, a forlorn-looking little figure too unhappy even to call for the attention she normally craved, much less try to alter the human's mood.

He sighed. He had signaled his coming and knew Islaen had been aware of him before he had stepped from the ladder, but she did not lift her head or otherwise acknowledge his presence, not even by so much as raising shields against him.

Islaen?

She looked up at last. *Aye?*

I was navigating right off the charts. I shall stay with the Maid *when we planet, as you suggest.*

Her head lowered. *Is that what you want?*

What I want is irrelevant.

The Commando looked at him. He meant precisely that.

No, that's never true. We've both had to sacrifice our own desires often enough, but it's not a law of the universe, and I don't think it's necessary this time. Hadesim know very well that the populations of a great many planets could pass for their oppressors. You couldn't stay long without trouble maybe, but for a single, short-term visit, your uniform and official purpose should be more than sufficient to protect you if you still wish to go. Besides, our assignment won't be much affected even if you do get into a fight and are forced to withdraw.

I wish to go, he replied slowly. *That has not changed.* He seemed to look past her, through her, for an instant. *My reasons are not sufficient to excuse insubordination—*

Stop it, Varn! I made just as much of an ass of myself as you did. Her eyes closed, as if with great weariness. *Please hold me, will you?*

Sogan slid into the seat beside her and folded her into his arms. *Islaen . . .*

I shouldn't have pulled rank on you. I was only playing the coward. I'd seen you come close, too close, to death so many times, and I couldn't bear the thought of possibly losing you for no true reason at all.

Varn's arms tightened around her and his lips brushed the smoldering fire of her auburn hair. He poured his love into her, reassuring and thanking her both.

His carefully shielded thoughts were dismal. Even in her failings this woman was sublime, while he . . . She had not even questioned him as to why he wanted to go to Hades of Persephone so badly.

For one instant he thought to tell her so that she would at least realize that he did have a reason, however warped, for setting himself against her.

That impulse died as it was born. Such a confession was impossible, inconceivable. He had endured much in his life, enough to break the mind and soul of many a man, but he could not bear Islaen Connor's contempt and dared not risk drawing that down upon himself.

FIVE

SOGAN STARTED AND jerked his head back as Bandit suddenly darted between him and the tape reader. Islaen's laughter sounded in his mind.

You were oblivious to us when you went up to the bridge, and you were still oblivious when we came back, so she decided to recall you to the real universe. She hates being ignored, you know.

He flexed his shoulders and was surprised to find how tense his muscles were. *I was going over your tapes on Hades,* he told her grimly. *She is no paradise by the look of it.*

No, she agreed. *Those who first-shipped to her deserve credit. They didn't have an easy time of it establishing themselves.*

Her look took on a devilishly mischievous cast, and Varn braced himself.

What do you think of our proposed route? she asked casually.

I am hardly in a position to complain, Colonel, he remarked noncommittally.

She laughed again. *Complain away, Admiral. I'm not exactly happy about it myself.*

The way I see it, we do not have a route, merely a listing of potential hazards.

She shook her head. *Do you realize that there are actually some people who consider caving, as they call it, a sport?*

So your tapes indicate, but then, Arcturians have always known that Terrans and their offshoots are more than a little mad.

Yes, Bandit interjected. *Bandit doesn't like this.*

"Why?" Varn asked. "You can fly, and so need not fear a fall, and places too tight for us are still vast halls for you."

Islaen and Varn might get stuck. Besides, gurries don't like dark, cold holes. —Jade's pretty now, she added hopefully. *Let's go there instead.*

"Sorry love," Islaen answered. "It's got to be Hades for us."

Her mind touched the man's again. *I'm about to program the range for some dinner. Are you ready to eat as well?*

Aye. I can finish reading what little remains later on. I shall join you in a few minutes.

As soon as his companions had left him, Sogan dismantled the reader and returned it and the tapes to their places. He did not think to leave it where it was, although he would probably be returning to it again within the hour. Equipment was not left unattended on a starship where mishaps could occur with alarming suddenness and small, loose items could too easily become potentially deadly missiles.

He paused as he closed the final tape in its case. He was not looking forward to this venture. A spacer could spend a great part of his life in areas far more tightly confined than any passage they might be called upon to utilize beneath Hades' crust, but his mind was attuned to vast panoramas, to distance and infinite emptiness, to an absence of apparent physical boundaries. This other kind of darkness—the close, crushing weight of a world's bones above and all around—was something entirely alien, unpleasant to contemplate, and nothing he had any wish to experience.

Islaen had as much as told him that she did not care for the idea of journeying into Hades' underworld, either, but her case was different. She and Jake Karmikel were both accustomed to working on-world, and their Commando training had at least familiarized them with the techniques and equipment they would be called upon to use. He had no such skills or foreknowledge to back him. . . .

The former Admiral sighed and headed for the *Maid*'s tiny mess. What lay ahead might not prove to be enjoyable, but it was no impossible task either. A presumably equally untrained Navy technician had made the same journey blindfolded before the invasion of Hades in order to reassemble

and arm that accursed planetbuster. He might be less than a
Commando in such a situation, but he was surely a match for
that other Federation warrior.

Islaen Connor, Varn Tarl Sogan, and their Jadite companion were standing before the near-space viewer on the bridge
of the *Fairest Maid*. Their attention was fixed on the rust-red
planet filling most of the screen.

She looks like Mars of Sol, if you discount the atmosphere,
the Commando remarked.

Aye.

Sogan was studying Hades of Persephone even as Orlan
Fran Uskorn might have studied her that day decades before,
when he had prepared to take his fleet in to seize her.

She was a harsh world, he knew, but not nearly so desertlike
as she appeared from space. There were several fairly large
rivers down there which distance rendered invisible, and her
opposite face supported two shallow seas. Her surface was
extremely porous, however, and most of her considerable
volume of water flowed far beneath her visible face, only
occasionally rising enough to bubble forth in springs such as
those supporting life in Karst and the few other major
communities.

The action of that subsurface water over the countless eons
had riddled all the crust with interconnecting caves and caverns, some several thousand feet deep, and at least two
systems extending over a thousand miles in length. Only the
smallest portion of them, those closest to the population
centers, had been even superficially explored.

As for the planet's life, humans and the livestock and
crops they had brought with them accounted for most of it
aboveground. There were a few photosynthetic plants near the
various water sources on the surface and some animal species, none of them large, utilizing them, but most of the red
planet's native offspring dwelled far from Persephone's light,
in deep caves where each plant and animal was a link in a complex, mutually supportive ecological chain nearly as old as
life itself on Hades. All the animals were cold-blooded and
quite small, although many existed in enormous numbers.

"Bandit is right," he said aloud. "Jade has far more to
offer."

"She does indeed," Islaen agreed. "It'll be great seeing Jake again, though. I wonder if he's planeted yet."

"Probably. He was a lot closer to Hades to start with, even with the *Maid*'s speed."

Islaen's eyes darkened with concern. "I hope he's up to this. It'll be strenuous at best, and he'll never have the sense to keep out of it. He was pretty badly cut up. . . ."

Varn gave her a look of mock disgust. "He was fine before we ever left Jade."

She sighed. "I know. I guess I worry too much at times."

"I shall not challenge that, Colonel."

His smile was tender. He knew that she and Karmikel had entered Basic at the same time from the planet Noreen, had undergone Commando training together and then had served in the same unit throughout the War. The mere fact of Karmikel's return to civilian status could hardly be expected to lessen the bond between them. Not even his own marriage with her could do that.

His mind touch was soft. *Be easy, Islaen Connor. You shall soon know. I will inquire about the* Jovian Moon *when I request planeting permission, and if she is on-world, I shall ask Jake to come to us as soon as we are down.*

SIX

JAKE KARMIKEL'S STARSHIP had planeted the previous morning. No sooner had Sogan set his needle-nose down and lifted her space seals than the Noreenan man requested permission to board.

That was quickly granted, and minutes later, he enveloped Islaen in an exuberant bear hug.

Varn watched the two comrades for a moment. Amused by their uninhibited greeting, he chuckled. "If you do not let her go, you will crack her ribs."

Jake complied, grinning broadly. "I'll spare you the same treatment, Admiral, but I'm right glad to see you as well."

The woman smoothed her rumpled tunic. "To think I was worried you mightn't be yourself yet!" she grumbled.

"Nothing like giving a little actual proof of health and well-being," he told her. "Ah, there's my little girl!"

He reached Bandit in two strides. The gurry had taken refuge on the Arcturian's shoulder during the turmoil of the redhead's entrance, but was now whistling loudly for her share of his attention.

She purred happily under his stroking. He well knew how to please a gurry by now. Most of Jade's settlers had paired with the tiny mammals, and he had plenty of practice in catering to them.

At first a rare smile played on Varn's lips, but then he frowned. Did he make such a fool of himself with Bandit?

Islaen's laughter broke into his thoughts.

No, you don't. Not even a gurry can soften Varn Tarl Sogan that much, unfortunately.

Unfortunately? He started to look sharply at her but caught her devilry and only shook his head, his own eyes dancing. He was not going to let her bait him this time.

Once more he frowned, a heaviness seeping into his spirit. He carefully slipped his shields into place to conceal it. The Commando had spoken in jest, but perhaps he should accept that mock reprove as real. What sort of man—or half man—was he anyway? he wondered savagely. He could not play with a gurry. He could not even greet his own wife the way this man did. . . .

At least Islaen was occupied with the other two and was not aware of his thoughts—or of the fact that he had thoughts he wished to keep veiled from her.

She let Karmikel go on for another few seconds, then interrupted him. "Jake, Bandit might want you to continue like this indefinitely, but we do have a reason for being here. Where's the demolitions expert?"

"Outside on the boarding ramp. She knows we're old friends, and preferred to let us do our greeting in private."

He anticipated her next question. "Our guide wants no part of starships. He took an office in one of the port buildings and will meet us there. He wants to check our gear and take us below as soon as possible. Needless to say, everyone here's anxious to have that planetbuster neutralized."

"I would be anxious as well if this were my city," Varn agreed. "Go with Jake and make the woman welcome, Islaen. I shall finish securing the *Maid* and then join you."

"Well and good. We'll pick up our packs on our way down."

The Colonel and her former teammate paused at the cargo level to retrieve the packs she had assembled after being briefed about her mission.

Jake nodded in appreciation when he saw that there were four. "Two of them are for us?"

"Aye, of course." She frowned. "Your passenger will be able to handle it?"

He nodded. "She should if the rest of us can. None of us have any underground experience."

"True enough."

The Commando started to go, but his hand stopped her. "Islaen, Ram Sithe briefed us via transceiver. Hades of Persephone is no place for our Admiral. No off-worlders are really welcome here, but the locals aren't going to like having him around at all."

"I know."

"So why in space—"

"Because he wants to come."

"Why?" Karmikel demanded bluntly. "His real place is in space. He'll be at a disadvantage compared to the two of us underground, and if I know anything about him, he realizes that and can't like it."

"He hasn't chosen to tell me."

"Well, that's in keeping with an Arcturian war prince right enough," he replied in disgust. "You should've married me, like I wanted, lass."

"I have a feeling life wouldn't be very much simpler."

The Noreenan man silently cursed himself. He had meant that in jest, and Islaen had responded exactly as he had imagined she would, but it struck him suddenly that the former Admiral's reticence might in fact be troubling to her. If that were the case, his remark had been in decidedly poor taste.

Better just let it go, he reasoned. She knew him well enough to realize that he had meant no ill.

"Wait until you meet Bethe Danlo," he said hastily as they began their descent again. "She's all right. She was Regular service, of course, but one doesn't get hidebound in her line of work."

"I imagine not," Islaen agreed dryly. "She's space-bred, I believe."

"Aye, for generations. She carries Terran citizenship, so her line must've originated there, as if her face wouldn't be enough to tell one that."

They fell silent as they reached the entry hatch where the woman they had been discussing was waiting, leaning casually on the rail of the boarding ramp.

She was very small and proportionally slender, with thin, pleasant features of a more or less purely Terran cast. The fine, golden-blonde hair was worn in a coronet pinned tightly to her head, even as Islaen's was, the almost universal style adopted by women who ranged the starlanes. Her eyes were a slate blue. They had a steady look about them, an assurance that bespoke the willingness and ability to face the challenges fate sent.

Bethe frankly studied Islaen. She had visited Jade of Kuan Yin often enough to know that the surprisingly lovely Commando officer was a legend there, twice the savior of the people colonizing that world. She was also already well on the way to becoming an interstellar legend, as were the freighter captain she had married and, of course, Jake Karmikel. The prospect of working with the three of them was exciting, but it was also a little daunting.

Islaen returned her scrutiny, then smiled and extended her hand. "I'm Commando-Colonel Islaen Connor. Welcome to the *Fairest Maid*."

"Thanks. Bethe Danlo, formerly Sergeant Danlo."

"I know. Demolitions Unit." The guerrilla gave a shudder that was in no way exaggerated. "It's a job I wouldn't have liked to tackle. What we had to do in that line was more than sufficient to scare us off taking on any more."

Bethe laughed. "Nothing ever scared Commandos! Everyone knows that!"

Her mood sobered, and she shook her head. "I never thought I'd be working with any of you, especially after being out of uniform for the last four years."

Islaen smiled. "Don't be expecting any high heroics from us, or from this business, either, unless you supply them yourself when we reach the missile. This isn't really a Commando mission at all. Mostly, I was chosen for it because I happen to have both a high rank and some wilderness ability. It should be just a quick, straightforward job. The hardest part'll be the journey to and from—"

She broke off as she felt Varn's mind touch and, an instant later, saw him appear in the hatch.

"Bethe Danlo, this is Navy Captain Varnt Sogan, master of the *Fairest Maid*."

A chill ran through the very core of the demolitions expert's being. She had seen men like this before, the ranking

officers of the Arcturian Empire who had represented their
defeated ultrasystem at the signing of the surrender treaty. . . .

A sharp whistle suddenly disrupted her thoughts, and
she became aware of the small creature riding on the newcomer's shoulder. Her eyes widened and softened in the same
instant.

"A gurry!" she exclaimed in delight. "I didn't think those
Amonites would let any of them off-world!"

She stopped herself. That might be true as far as all the rest
of the Federation's population went, but these two would be
exempt from that rule and from any other. If they wanted it,
half Jade would cheerfully be signed over to them.

"They're right too," she added fiercely as she timidly
reached out to the apparently eager hen. "Given our species'
record, it's better not to risk their being neglected or abused
or locked up in some vile lab."

Bethe looked up at the Captain. Amusement softened his
harsh features, gentled them in a way that was both unexpected and pleasing, and she found herself liking him.

She stepped back hastily. "I'm sorry, Captain. I shouldn't
have—"

"Nonsense. Bandit could live on attention. —Take her for a
moment, if you like."

As he spoke, the gurry flitted from his shoulder to the
woman's hands.

Islaen drew a deep breath of relief as she linked her thoughts
with Varn's. *That was too close.*

She did know?

She made a connection. I could feel her shock.

The Commando could not join with other minds as she did
with this man's or the gurry's, but she could read strong
emotion and general feeling more than well enough to recognize their danger in this encounter.

So did Bandit, fortunately, she added in obvious relief. *I
believe she has the situation well in hand, for the moment at
least.*

Sogan nodded almost imperceptibly. Gurries had the facil-
ity of transmitting enormous concentrations of goodwill to
those around them. That was the secret of the extraordinary
effect they had upon humans, all save the most debased or

those so caught in the grip of some emotion as to be unreachable by any other. The power of this influence extended to the gurries' adopted partners as well, moving others to respond favorably to them. Now the spacer would very likely judge Varn for himself, as she saw him, not by any imagined past or in accordance with any stereotype.

He glanced at Karmikel, but Jake had apparently missed the brief crisis entirely. He was absorbed in watching the blond woman's delight.

Varn's eyes held a grim look when they joined with his consort's as he slid past her to begin descending the ramp.

That could have been bad, especially in this place, he muttered, then apologized. *Even my so-called alias could give us away.*

Now that the time of potential confrontation was almost upon them, he was beginning to feel guilty about his earlier stubbornness.

That's not your fault, Islaen told him firmly. *Varn, you're not bound to this,* she said sympathetically. *Jake's not radiating any good feeling about these characters. If they're likely to be a problem, you don't have to deal with them.*

I know, but let it go on for now, until it seems to become threatening.

That's reasonable enough.

She felt relieved at his more tractable mood, and it was with a lighter heart that she followed him to the small four-wheeler Jake had brought with him.

What do you think of Bethe? Islaen asked.

A smile flickered on his lips. *She likes gurries.*

Varn!

I do not know. Her record is outstanding, according to your tapes, and I like what I see. If she is as good as she seems, we should have a smooth glide.

His thoughts stilled, and a darkness settled over him. His consort looked to him with some concern.

What's wrong, Varn? If something seems off, we'd do better to play with it.

Not off. . . . He flushed but went on. *It is just an attack of pure superstition,* he admitted frankly. *We have been making little of this assignment, yet that has not been our experience with any of the work that has come to us thus far.*

You're thinking maybe we're issuing a rather unwise challenge to fortune, or to whatever gods rule Hades?

She did not laugh. Sogan was embarrassed, as he always was when he admitted to some weakness, and she did not want to add to his discomfort. Besides, he had touched an unhappy spark in her own heart.

Don't even imagine it, my friend. We've proven adept enough at drawing problems to us without any outside help, material or otherwise.

SEVEN

THE FOUR CROSSED Hades' fine planeting field in short order and came to a halt before an office complex, a building containing individual rooms and suites, some permanently occupied, others available for use by visitors to the port.

"We've got one on the second level," Jake informed them. "Greggs is there, or at least he should be by now."

Islaen let him and the other woman go up first. She matched her step to Varn's. As they reached the top of the ramp, her mind receptors linked with his so that he would share in whatever information she received from the individual they could see waiting for them in the brightly lit room beyond.

Larnse Greggs was a small man by Federation standards, although of better than average height amongst his own people. He had what she called a hatchet face, sharp and hard, with small, pale blue eyes that seemed incapable of mirroring a smile. His skin had a blue cast as well, the mark of a Hadesi, which somehow jarred with his unruly mop of straw-colored hair. His body was slender and straight. It was well although tensely held, and there was nothing furtive in the way his gaze sought and held those of the two off-worlders already in the room with him.

He nodded to the Commando as she stepped into the office from the shadowed hall.

Then he saw Varn.

The kind of warfare waged on Hades had honed the reactions of her surviving offspring to almost instantaneous speed. Even as hatred exploded from his mind, a blaster was appearing in his hand.

37

Varn Tarl Sogan, through his link with Islaen, had felt that
savage outburst and the hunger for blood accompanying it.
The warning did not come soon enough for him to draw his
own weapon in time to meet the other's attack, but he had
effective alternatives to armed combat.

He sprang forward rather than back. Even as he reached the
other, his hand shot out and down, striking the Hadesi's wrist
with numbing force, driving the blaster from his hold in the
moment he fired it. The bolt went wild, searing the wall only
inches to the left of its intended target.

Larnse recovered fast, but before he could deliver a
counterstrike, a crackling stream of flaming energy tore through
the narrow strip of air separating the two men.

"Freeze, both of you!" Islaen Connor commanded.

They obeyed, Varn with a great sense of relief.

The guerilla officer started to move cautiously toward Greggs,
covered by Jake's weapon, but to her surprise, Bethe reached
him first.

She shoved him hard and, with the Hadesi off balance,
succeeded in flinging him against the scorched wall.

"What in the name of space is the matter with you?" she
demanded furiously.

"That—thing is an Arcturian," he hissed venomously, the
will to death still plain in his eyes, although the means of
fulfilling it had been temporarily torn from him.

"You planet-hugging microwit! None of their kind were
exactly good losers. Why should any of them come back here
to a scene of their defeat? On top of that, when did you ever
hear of one of them carting a little beastie around. They don't
even hate animals; they ignore them completely."

It was a good move, Islaen thought, whether it was inten-
tional or not. The enraged man's attention had been turned to
the gurry, and right now she was a sight enough to hold it.

The Jadite mammal was in midair, halfway between the
former Admiral and his would-be assassin. Her feathers were
extended to the full, and she was hissing so strongly in her
fury that the sound was slightly painful to human ears.

Greggs glared at her for several seconds, his anger driven
to an even higher pitch, then the utterly ludicrous nature of
the confrontation broke full upon him. He gave one more

look at Sogan's minute defender, and the ghost of a smile touched his lips despite his effort to suppress it.

"All right," he growled. "Call off your pet. I'm no more danger to you. For now, anyway."

Keep it up, love. You're doing fine, Islaen's mind whispered, although she knew from the fierce lash of hatred radiating from the man that Bandit had little chance of softening him.

Her voice was like the crack of a force whip when she turned to Larnse. "Are you aware that I could haul you off to Horus for military trial? This man is not only a Federation citizen but a Navy officer here on official assignment!"

"Federation citizen!" he spat. "What planet does he claim—"

"Both Thorne of Brandine and Jade of Kuan Yin," she replied evenly. "Not that I am required to answer you."

Varn interrupted, addressing both of them. "I am aware that the citizens of Hades have good cause for their hostility to the Empire's representatives, and my appearance has caused me similar trouble in the past. I have even drawn upon it for our benefit. If Mr. Greggs will refrain from making further attempts on my life, I am prepared to forget this incident and get on with our business. I do not think any of us wants to remain on Hades longer than absolutely necessary."

"Well, Mr. Greggs?" Colonel Connor asked.

He hesitated only a moment. Bandit had resumed her perch on the dark-eyed man's shoulder, and the sight of her there seemed to reassure him.

"I agree. Karst's safety must stand before anything else."

"That is understood." Islaen took a deep breath. "Have there been any further moves by the pirates or their agents?"

"Possible agents," Larnse corrected, but he went on at once. "There never was anything definite from them, but even the possibility must be countered."

"Everything except the planetbuster has been returned?"

He nodded. "Aye, and properly stored, but our people didn't dare touch the big one."

"You were wise there," Bethe told him. "They're tricky, especially those old ones."

Varn stirred restlessly. *Islaen, can this man be trusted? We have seen he is quick to slay. If we were to die underground, and with us the only demolitions expert in the area, pirates could move in and be off with the missile before your Navy could fly in replacements.*

I know, but his hate's still overriding just about every other emotion. I can't get enough of a grip on anything else to read him deeper. —Can you provoke him, force him to bring up something more?

I can try. His cold eyes fixed the Hadesi.

"That planetbuster could be removed without damage to Karst and used elsewhere," Varn said, "on a planet with the resources to make blackmail worthwhile, for example. Why do you not just let the wolf pack take it, since you so patently resent dealing with off-worlders?"

The Hadesi answered with such a wave of fury that both Varn and Islaen had to physically brace themselves not to reel back under it.

"I saw butcherwork in plenty and hated the butchers!" Larnse snarled. "I won't be of one kind with them, not even by refusing to act."

"At least one of your people may have decided otherwise," Bethe Danlo said slowly.

"Not me!" He calmed himself with difficulty. "You have a right to an answer. If true, it's a disgrace to all Hades and to me personally. Geord's blood kin of mine, the only such remaining to me and the only other member of my Resistance cell to survive."

His voice had grown thick, and he forced it to harden again. "Loss and pain leave their scars. Hades is a bitter world at best, and where destruction was complete, sometimes total brutalization followed, with only an interest in bringing pain or in personal gain left to fuel the continuation of an individual's life. I don't know if this is the case here. My kinsman has vanished and is not available for examination, but I think it may be likely. His soul as well as his heart bled heavily."

The blond woman's head lowered. "Aye, that could well be. I've seen that too."

Islaen's eyes flickered toward Varn. Reason demanded that this should be the case with the former Admiral, yet instead he had come forth a man so fine . . .

She felt his question and quickly sealed off that part of her thoughts. *His motive's sound.* She paused. *So is his grief. His losses have been heavy, and I think he still bears love for this renegade.*

Possible renegade. —Aye, so do I read it, but I am not yet as sure of my interpretations as you. She felt his mental grimace. *My feelings are against the man as well. I fear they may be coloring my impressions.*

No, you're reading fairly.

Islaen's attention seemed never to have wavered from the Hadesi. "Your leaders were wise to want to get that thing away from here. When can we start?"

"As soon as I assure myself that you're properly equipped. Where we shall be journeying, anything less is death."

"We've brought our packs. Our gear is standard Federation caving equipment, plus arms and items belonging to our own work, some of which remain classified."

"I needn't see those as long as I approve of the way they're stowed."

Islaen touched her pack with the toe of her boot. "I've got a renewer in here. It fits, but it's bulky."

The Hadesi sent a swift glance downward. "That small?" he asked in amazement.

She nodded. "Aye. Hand operable. They're just about brand new. We didn't have anything like them during the War. In fact, Jade's settlers got the first batch for testing. I requisitioned this after seeing them in use there."

"You'll get no argument from me about that, Colonel. I wish every mining team on Hades had one."

"That may be possible soon, if these continue to test out as well as they have thus far."

Islaen was hardly surprised over his excitement. Even after all this time, renewers were still one of medical science's greatest miracles, producing almost instantaneous, complete regeneration of damaged and destroyed skin, muscles, blood vessels, even nerves and bone. Only the organs of the chest and abdominal cavities could not be so repaired, requiring treatment with the much newer and far more complex re-growth equipment.

At the War's beginning only a few of the greatest experimental hospitals could support the then-massive renewer systems, but development had progressed quickly until they became standard on every major battleship, and then on the medium and many of the smaller-class vessels as well. Now, Federation scientists had produced a model usable by individuals or small, mobile parties.

Larnse said nothing more as he began his examination of the equipment. It was a thorough one, and only when he had finished did he address Islaen again.

"I can't fault any of this. It's much the same as we use, and all of it appears to be high quality. —Any of you experienced underground?"

"No," Jake Karmikel answered. "Commandos get a lot of mountain training, however. The techniques are similar; you folks just use them upside down."

Greggs chuckled. "With some differences, space hound."

He looked to the Colonel rather than at Sogan. "What about the other two?"

"They're tyros," she admitted, "but they've made it in space. Both have to be tough and adaptable."

"We'll see." His pale eyes went slowly from one to the other of them, as if measuring each.

"The way we're going presents relatively little hazard," he explained, "apart from one crossing where we might run into real trouble, but it's a physically hard haul nearly the whole way. We'll be five days going and probably longer coming back, since we'll be loaded down. Resign yourselves to a lot of work."

Bethe Danlo frowned. He had been looking at her as he spoke, and she guessed that her apparent lack of muscle had drawn that warning from him.

"You can count on us to lug our own weight."

"Maybe. In your case it doesn't matter anyway. You're our chief piece of equipment."

"Well, don't worry. You won't have to tote me!" she snapped. "All right, I'm small, and maybe I can't heft as much as you others, but I've been manhandling cargo since I was ten, and you can believe that machines and automatics don't do anything like half that work on the rim!"

Jake laughed. "Power down, firebrand. You may regret those words later."

Greggs shrugged and put the matter from his mind. She had been warned. Hades' women were small as well and functioned effectively. There was no reason why this off-worlder should not.

"We'll leave just before dawn. Those space togs are too light for this work," he added. "Wear heavy, strong clothes capable of standing up to abuse. Temperatures usually range between forty-seven and fifty degrees Fahrenheit, and our caves are nearly invariably damp. Your knee pads are good enough, but I'll supply the helmets. They're designed to take our lamps."

Islaen nodded. "I thought you might."

She concealed the feeling of discomfort that decision engendered in her. Hades' cave lamps were the most efficient in the ultrasystem, according to the tapes she had reviewed, and they were used on many other planets with heavy mining operations.

They functioned very simply on an energy current produced when two natural variants of the same substance, common here and rare elsewhere—florase A and florase Z—were brought into near but not actual contact. The liquids were contained in paper-thin, flexible plastisteel coils which carried the energy they generated and released it as light in the brilliant reflector globe fixed in the usual fashion on the upper front of the helmet.

The system was simple and worked well, but if the coils ever ruptured and the A and Z florase should physically meet, a powerful acid was produced. Because accidents could and did happen underground, the helmets were multilayered to provide maximum protection and were fashioned entirely of one of the few materials impervious to the acid. Still, there was something in her that shrank from even potential contact with the substance. . . .

Suddenly, laughter sounded in her mind.

This from a guerrilla who lives with all sorts of deadly items always at her side?

She answered Sogan with a single, biting word in his own language before giving her attention back to the Hadesi.

"Is there anything else, Mr. Greggs?"

"Your boots. Those must be changed as well."

This time Islaen was surprised. "Why? What's wrong with them? They provide good grip on a variety of surfaces and give both support and protection."

"Aye, but they're too hard. Hades' underground is not merely a harsh realm, but is in places a very beautiful one. Many of the formations gracing it have been countless eons in the making. They're our heritage and are more our treasure than any mineral we mine for export. We're not about to risk damage to them from heavy-footed off-worlders."

She inclined her head in assent. "A most understandable determination. —Very well, Mr. Greggs, we shall be back here an hour before Persephone rises."

Jake Karmikel dropped his former commander and her companion beside the *Fairest Maid* and then started for his own crescent-shaped starship.

Once they had drawn a little away from the *Maid*, he glanced at the demolitions expert sitting quietly beside him. "You moved fast in there," he said. "Thanks."

"Greggs is right, of course. This so-called Varnt Sogan is an Arcturian, and I'd say he carries a fairly respectable rank."

"You disproved that yourself," the former Commando remarked casually.

Bethe shot him a contemptuous look. "Damn it, man! I served with the honor guard at the surrender ceremonies. I know what Arcturians look like! Why Sogan's here, I don't know, but he's got his reasons and probably his orders for pairing up with you two. I'd say his feeling for the gurry is likely genuine since she defended him so vehemently, however he came to forget his kind's hard nature to yield to it."

The Noreenan kept his voice very quiet, as if he were only engaging her in a conversation of no real moment. "If you believe that, why did you come to his rescue?"

"Because that man's not a collective anything. He's himself, and I happen to know something of what he's been doing here. After that business on Visnu and then Astarte and Jade, I wouldn't care if he were a war prince or even one of the Emperor's chief combat Admirals. I wouldn't care if he were the Emperor himself. He's earned his place here."

Jake studied her. She meant that, he thought with something akin to awe.

"Bethe, Sogan has left his past. It was a hard one, and neither Islaen nor I will draw it back down on him, but I'll

tell you this much, there's nothing to shame him in it and
nothing to shame us in working with him."

"That I believe, Jake Karmikel," she said softly, "strongly
enough that I'm willing to stand as his friend." She sighed.
"He may be needing a few before this is all over."

Varn Tarl Sogan had held silent both outwardly and in his
mind during the short drive to the *Maid,* but once they were
aboard, he steeled himself to face the Commando officer.

*I should never have taken part in that meeting. It is my
fault that Greggs is soured on the lot of us.*

*Not entirely. He doesn't care for any Navy personnel. He
can't and won't forget that we gave Hades no help in her
torment.*

He shook his head in a gesture more of despair than denial.
He was the cause of it, whatever she said to spare him. Had
he not surrender to that original unworthy fear . . .

It was too late to rectify that.

What now? he asked wearily.

For you?

Aye.

*I said I wouldn't give you any orders about this. That
hasn't changed.*

Islaen's eyes fixed on him despite her statement. An order
from her should not be necessary. Varn knew what should be
done.

He did know, but he could not force the words from his
lips. His head lowered and he turned away from her. Suddenly he feared he could no longer screen what lay inside
him, and his shields snapped closed around his thoughts.

"If you command me to remain behind, I shall obey," he
told her through tightly set lips, "but of my own self, I
cannot. My courage is not sufficient."

Sogan tried to take hold of himself. His own need should
mean nothing when a clear duty was before him, but he could
not set it aside. Having failed so wretchedly in that, and
having damned himself doubly by confessing his failure, he at
least owed it to her to tell her the rest of it.

"Larnse Gregg's hatred is not logical. We both felt that.
He is hostile to me not because he knows I am an Arcturian,
but because I look like one. If I do not accompany you, his

anger may not die but rather become focused elsewhere. You are the most likely target because you team with me, and more so because you have taken me for your consort.''

He paused for a moment and then went on. ''I remember what it was like looking on while that renegade goldbeast almost killed you. I shall go insane if I have to follow your danger through mind link and maybe experience your death in some lightless hole, with the bones of a world keeping me from reaching even your body.''

For one instant so brief as almost not to be, his control faltered, and Islaen Connor knew what horror that possibility was for him.

His guards were back in place again even as they fell, but they had been down long enough to form and firm her own decision. She had sworn after their battle with that mad bull that she would never again force him to withdraw from her work. Varn had not called on her to hold to her word, but she could never refuse him now. For a war prince to beg . . .

She lay a small hand on his arm. ''Oh, Varn, I want you with me. You have to know that. Trouble may come of it, but you're right, we could have to face that anyway and in less predictable form.''

She looked at him so sharply that he was startled out of the dark cloud enveloping him.

What is it? he asked.

I may be sacrificing you down there.

In what way?

By making you the focus of Greggs's ill will if it should go out of control again. The pressure'd be off the rest of us, but things could be very unpleasant for you, if not actually dangerous.

He smiled, feeling almost physically weak with relief. A difficulty which might never materialize seemed so light a penalty to pay as to scarcely exist at all.

It is a risk worth the taking, Colonel Connor.

EIGHT

VARN SHIFTED IN an attempt to find a more comfortable position. The springless board that was the center seat of the six-wheeler carrying them to their entrance into Hades' underworld had not been made for the ease of its passengers.

Islaen and Larnse Greggs were in the front; Jake and the spacer woman had taken the place behind him, while their packs and some additional gear the Hadesi had brought lay in the transport's ample cargo space in the back.

Soon, now, they would reach the place from which they would make their descent. The Arcturian again went over in his mind the list of equipment the tapes had noted as essential for anyone venturing into a planet's crust. Anything forgotten could be retrieved at this point at no greater cost than some lost time and minor embarrassment. Later, the penalties might prove drastically higher.

Everything was there within quick and easy reach, stowed on his belt, in the pack, or in the various pockets of his sturdy garments.

His clothes, like the rest of his gear, were of a type developed over literally centuries of such work, heavy for warmth, strong enough to withstand wear and to grant protection from scrapes and abrasions, basically comfortable and nonrestrictive. They differed enough from the lighter garments used in space that he had not yet completely accustomed himself to the feel of them on his body, but that sensation should soon fade with continued use, and the more immediate concerns that would soon dominate his attention.

In truth, Sogan in one sense preferred this costume to the

one he had worn the previous evening. He had freely sworn allegiance to the Federation and willingly served its cause, but he had fought this ultrasystem for nearly the whole of his life, and he doubted he would ever feel completely at ease in its uniform.

The war prince closed off that line of thought with considerable annoyance. He had better use for his mind than pondering trivialities.

He had learned caution on Thorne, where every shadow might shelter a Resistance fighter, and now his eyes seemed to darken beyond their own near blackness as they scanned the rugged, broken landscape they were passing through. A small army with a minimum of skill could lie concealed out there amongst those red, gaunt hills, and its victims would never be the wiser until it struck to sweep them away.

Islaen, if my forces had not taken care to avoid places such as this on Thorne, little of my fleet would have remained at the surrender. Are you certain we are alone?

We're nothing like alone, her mind responded promptly. *There's a full company at least in those rocks up ahead. They're alert and curious, but I'm not picking up any hostility.*

Her assurances notwithstanding, the Commando turned to Larnse. "I thought it was unwritten law that no one goes into a cave without a surface backup in case of trouble."

"We've got one," he answered promptly and with an unwilling respect for what he took to be her good sense. "My people are here now. They know when we're due back and will come in after us if we don't show. They'll also see to it that no other parties follow us down," he added significantly. "That's why they're not showing themselves even to us. No use giving our safeguards away."

She nodded approvingly. "No use whatsoever. —You Hadesim handle yourselves well, Larnse Greggs."

"We've had to, Colonel," he replied stiffly, both pleased and nettled by the compliment.

Jake Karmikel relaxed. Islaen had managed that masterfully, as usual, and he saw that she was satisfied with their guide's answer, and that, and the readings her particular gift allowed her to take while he was speaking.

For his own part, the former guerrilla was almost sorry this was the case. Potential ambush was a concrete concern, and now that it was laid to rest, he had to set himself to face more phantasmagoric fears.

He felt angry, furious with himself. There was nothing before them that he was not fully capable of handling. He knew that, yet his unease continued to expand. He could not escape the feeling that he was about to enter into a completely alien realm, one quite inimical to him and all his kind.

That thought, all thought, ceased abruptly. He saw the place that was their goal.

A great, gaping blackness loomed before them, a huge mouth yawning in the steep side of a jagged cliff.

Could such a place be termed a cave at all? The *Fairest Maid* could have stood comfortably under that massive arch. His own squat little *Moon* would be utterly dwarfed there.

"Here's where we leave the machines," Larnse told them as he brought the transport to a halt just inside the mouth of the vast grotto.

He let them look their fill. It was awesome, beautiful with a harsh, stark grandeur. The loveliness of light and shadow was here, the power of sheer size, of slabs, each as large as a small building, interlocking so perfectly that they seemed no more than bricks carefully laid in an artistically haphazard pattern, albeit by the hands of giants. He was proud of his homeworld, and he knew by their expressions that the off-worlders appreciated this minor wonder of hers. They would soon be seeing some of her less favorable faces. Let them at least have the memory of this to stand against those.

At last he opened the door on his side and stepped down from the six-wheeler, signaling the others to follow.

They unloaded their gear, then stood looking for a few minutes into the darkness at the grotto's rear until their eyes had adjusted enough to penetrate it. Chiefly, they saw a continuation of the rugged walls and several huge slabs lying in a patently artificial semicircle around what seemed to be a patch of infinite blackness staining the cave's floor.

"We used those to conceal the entrance to the underworld, since it made too easy a road down," Greggs explained. "Not that our efforts proved necessary," he added contemptuously. "The Arcturians never even made a real search of the place . . . thought it was too open to hold any passages or to be of interest to the Resistance. —They didn't seem to like caves very much, anyway, not even big, lighted ones like this."

"You used other entrances yourselves, I presume," Sogan remarked carefully.

"Naturally. There are many, a number of them eventually leading to the depot, but they're hard to negotiate and would be impossible with the planetbuster."

The Hadesi looked from one to the other of them, as if daring them to back out. The harshness faded from him when his gaze fell on Bandit, and his hand raised to touch her in the universal manner of a human suddenly becoming aware of a gurry. Islaen Connor could feel the power flow from the hen as she strove to soften him even further.

"You shouldn't bring that little beast," he told her. "She'll be safe enough from most of the threats we'll face, but it's cold belowground, and the damp and dark might get to her."

Islaen managed not to wince as ten sharp claws clamped tightly on her shoulder in a grasp painful even through the thick material of her jacket.

Cut the violence, will you!

Bandit goes!

Not if you rip my shoulder open, she grumbled, but she smiled at the guide. "Don't worry about Bandit. Gurries developed on a temperate planet where they must endure considerable seasonal fluctuations in weather conditions. They're hardier than they seem, and she can ride inside my jacket if the chill starts to bite at her."

"Whatever you say," he replied doubtfully, "but I don't want to be held responsible for her getting sick. Lung fevers have always been common here."

Larnse strained to lift the first of two bulky packages he had brought with him. "Collapsible boats," he explained. "We get to ride for part of the trip. I'll lower them first, and then we can start going down ourselves. I'll make the initial descent, then the women. The men should follow after, since they're the biggest and heaviest, and therefore the most likely to get stuck or fall someplace. We shouldn't risk splitting the party if something like that were to happen."

Islaen shot a glance at Varn and shook her head firmly.

"No way, Mr. Greggs. Captain Sogan's my backup. He comes after me, then Bethe and Jake."

He shrugged. "If you insist."

The Hadesi moved to the edge of the gaping black pit. A long, flexible ladder had been placed there for their descent. He examined this carefully before securing it to a conveniently placed but quiet natural outcropping. He tested its fastenings and cast it into the seeming void. That done, he unwound the ropes already clipped to each of the two boats and gingerly began to let them down, first one, then the other, taking great care that they not strike against the walls of the chimney. The whole process seemed to take a discouragingly long time to the waiting off-worlders.

When both vessels were at last safely on the ground far below, he turned to the others. "We go down one at a time. Wait until I tug the ladder three times, then you start, Colonel. I'll shout when I'm ready as well, but voices carry poorly underground, so don't depend on hearing me for your signal."

With that, he swung himself over the edge.

The four humans restrained their curiosity and kept well back from the lip of the chimney lest they inadvertently knock debris on top of the slowly descending man. No such constraints held Bandit. She flew over the pit and then swooped some feet into it.

She returned after a few moments, calling with a shrill, displeased whistle as she settled onto the Colonel's shoulder. *Black, ugly place!*

You should have listened to us and stayed on the ship, Varn told her severely, using mind touch so that Bethe Danlo would not realize there was speech passing between them. *I do not think much of our guide, but he was right to say you should not go with us.*

Neither should Varn, the gurry replied.

The Arcturian stiffened. He fixed the Jadite creature with a furious stare.

His consort intervened before he could reply. *Let her be, Varn. You're going to look ridiculous if you let yourself be provoked into a fight with a gurry.*

He glared at them both, then turned away with his mind shields tightly in place, ostensibly to check his pack.

Islaen Connor set her own guards. She knew what the

former Admiral did not—that the little hen could read closed thoughts—and she lashed out at Bandit. *That was pretty damned stupid! I thought you knew better.*

But Varn shouldn't come—

He's aware of that fact. That's why he's mad.

Why does he want to come?

He hasn't deigned to say.

Now he doesn't want Bandit, the hen wailed miserably.

Don't be ridiculous. Even if you'd let him not want you, he loves you too much. It's only because he was concerned about you that he wanted you to stay behind in the first place.

Bandit's sorry, she said contritely.

She looked as miserable as the unhappiness she radiated, and Islaen sighed. *Maybe I'm just expecting too much from you, little Bandit, too much understanding of humans and human ways, but I do need your help. I have enough to do trying to watch what's happening between Varn and Greggs, and between Greggs and the rest of us, without having to worry about clashes in my own party. We can't afford that, love. It might be enough to kill us all.*

Bandit understands, the gurry replied slowly after a short silence. *I can fix.*

Wait until Varn cools down and then try to make up with him. —Don't be too sly about it, either. As long as he knows you're trying to manipulate him, he'll allow you do it, and even enjoy it, but if he comes to think you're working on him without his realizing you're there, he'll shut himself up behind shields so tight that an exploding star couldn't loosen them.

Bandit knows that, she declared indignantly.

A faint, incomprehensible shout reached Islaen's ears, and the ladder jerked sharply three times.

"That's my signal!" the Commando called to her companions. "Wish me luck," she added, then went to her knees and, turning, grasped the top of the ladder where it curved over the edge into the pit.

The gurry gave an alarmed squawk as she disappeared beneath the lip.

"Bandit!" Varn called sharply, then switched to mind speech. *Come here, you mind-delving little rogue. Do not distract her.*

He held his hand out to her, and the hen wheeled to claim the proffered perch, purring because he had forgiven and accepted her once more.

Islaen caught that part of their exchange and smiled, knowing there would be no ruffled feathers, figurative or literal, by the time she had finished her descent.

She frowned then. There should have been no ruffling in the first place, and she realized she herself was not guiltless in that respect. She had jumped Sogan several times recently without real or sufficient cause.

One thing for certain, she was going to push for that furlough Varn had mentioned when they got back to Horus. Visnu, Astarte, Jade, and now this mission, however minor it might be in itself—it was too much in too short a time span, especially with the terrible strain put on them by the stakes for which they had fought. It was beginning to tell on them. They needed a rest, a real rest, not just a few days like they had on Noreen after their marriage and the battle they had waged for Astarte's sake, and she was not about to see their morale and efficiency weakened for want of it.

Her face hardened momentarily. She would not permit what she and Varn Tarl Sogan had built between them to be weakened at all.

Islaen reached the bottom at last and looked around. It was something like being in a large bottle or funnel, she decided, for the narrow neck through which they had descended opened into a comfortably-sized little chamber. It was dark, but enough light filtered down the hundred-odd feet from the entrance to enable eyes grown accustomed to it to make out details.

Although her link with Varn's mind had already told him she was down and safe, she gave him the physical signals as well, first by calling to him and then by pulling on the ladder. That done, she looked up to watch him start. That scramble for the top rung was the trickiest part of the whole—

"Little fool, get over here!"

Larnse Greggs caught her roughly and hurled her back against the rugged, damp-stained wall.

Her mind and will were faster than her reflexes, fortu-

nately so. Even as her muscles had tensed to strike, she
realized that he didn't mean any harm. The Hadesi was
radiating a sharp concern and some triumph, not any sign of
treachery.

Islaen struck his hands sharply with the edges of her own,
breaking his hold. "Greggs, what in the name of space are
you about?" she demanded coldly.

"You don't stand under a descending caver, not if you can
help it. If he knocked anything loose or dropped something
from that height, it could smash your skull, helmet or not."

She nodded. "Thanks. I owe you that one. It won't happen
again."

He looked at her closely, with surprise and some respect.
He had not expected either this control or her acceptance that
he had been in the right.

He also realized his high-handed method of proving his
superiority in this situation might have backfired disastrously.
The ease with which she had snapped his hold was enough to
tell him that, fighter though he was, she could as readily have
cracked his neck had she been in less command of herself. It
was not a mistake he would repeat a second time.

Neither Jake Karmikel nor the blond woman beside him
had been aware of the exchange passing between their human
comrades and the gurry. Their own attention and interest were
fixed on the now invisible Hadesi.

Jake was filled with an almost heady sense of relief. He
had not known what he could expect to find here, and certainly did not know what to expect in the dark realm far
below, but the sight of the ladder had steadied him as only the
sudden appearance of the familiar in a totally alien situation
can do.

Spacers knew ladders, climbed them countless times every
day of their lives. If there were differences here, they were
too minute to cloud his mood.

Bethe Danlo felt the same way. She gave a great sigh as
the Arcturian vanished into the darkness, and smiled up at the
redhead. "It's like a good omen finding that here, isn't it?
Hades' gods seem to be telling us inner and outer space are
not so terribly different, merely two aspects of the same
universe."

"That's just about what I was thinking," he admitted, relieved that the demolitions expert had shared his unease. He did not feel like such a fool now.

She started to move toward the lip. "Sogan should be down soon, I suppose."

"Aye." He paused. "Be careful. That thing isn't a ship's ladder. The technique of climbing it's not the same."

She smiled. "I read the Colonel's tapes last night, too, and I'm not likely to forget their warnings, friend. It's a long way down to a very hard ground."

The signal came from Sogan, and Jake found himself waiting alone. He gave one final glance at the bright morning sky outside the grotto and then resolutely faced away from it. If he were going into darkness, he would do well to get his eyes adjusted to it as soon as possible.

At last it was time for him to begin. Karmikel squirmed into position to grasp the first rung. There was one heart-stopping instant of uncertainty, then he was climbing down, into Hades' sunless breast.

It was not a rapid descent such as he would have made aboard his *Moon*. Her ladders were rigid, firmly fixed in their places, and he slid more often than clambered down them. This one was flexible, moving in response to every motion he made, swaying and shivering perceptibly as he worked his way to its bottom.

His progress was steady if not fast, and he recognized the sense of the deliberate style of movement recommended and practiced by their guide—that of bringing his leg around the ladder at each step and inserting it from the back so that the heel of his boot would catch securely against the rung.

Finally he was down. Islaen's hand raised in welcome, then she turned to the Hadesi.

"What's next, Mr. Greggs?"

He gave each of them a measuring look. "We have several days' hard work in front of us, a lot more climbing and some crawling, but there are only two really difficult spots. One is dangerous. The other, which we are about to encounter, is merely unpleasant."

As he said the last, he pointed to what looked like a slit about a foot off the floor.

"That is the entrance to the maddest, most foolish passage

on all Hades, at least that we've discovered thus far. It's really more of a chamber, a bit short of sixty feet at its widest but at no point more than two feet high. Mostly the roof's a good two or three inches lower than that.''

"You say there's no danger?'' the guerrilla officer questioned doubtfully.

He shook his head. "None, Colonel, unless someone's stupid enough to take off his helmet and crack his head on the roof. It isn't even possible to get lost. A light is visible throughout the whole place, and there are only two exits.''

"Will there be room enough?'' asked Bethe. "You Hadesim are used to working underground. We aren't.''

"Plenty of room. Almost anyone can get through a space only one foot square. We'll have more space than we'll need to the sides, and the lowest point still gives us a foot and a half. No one'll get stuck.''

He glanced at the hole. "It's safe, and it's not terribly long as such passages can go, but we're not going to have any fun. The human body just doesn't like staying bent at that angle for any significant period of time.''

Larnse looked somberly at them. "If you want to back out, now's your chance. Otherwise, get set for twenty minutes of pure misery.''

NINE

VARN TARL SOGAN pushed his pack before him. Twenty minutes, Greggs had said. It seemed like they had been in this accursed crawlway for twenty years, and he knew they could not be half through it yet.

He glanced with real hatred at the red stone looming so close above him, hate and something else. This never-ending mass was cold, ugly, threatening. It seemed only to be waiting for the chance to crush out their lives. His eyes closed for a moment. It seemed almost eager to press down upon him, to press until not so much as atoms remained of what had once been his shell, as if Hades' own malignant spirit had somehow infused it with life and the lust for vengeance against all members of the race which had wrought such enormous ill here.

The Arcturian gripped himself. If he let his imagination run with him like this, he was done before they had even begun. He forced himself to study the surroundings dispassionately. Larnse Greggs had named this place a chamber, and so it was in one sense, for the stone roof and the floor lying so closely beneath it were both surprisingly smooth, almost as if they had been worked. There were irregularities, a nearly infinite number of them, revealed in the harsh beam of his lamp, but they all had an oddly rounded look. Water had done that, water that had flowed through here for countless years long eons past, until its course had been turned in some other direction or to some other level.

When would this end? Every muscle, every joint in his body was screaming with the torture of the unnatural half

crawl he was forced to mantain, but there seemed no relief
or hope of relief before him.

He looked up, straining to pierce the glow of his own lamp
to pick out the two circles of light reflecting from the rock not
far ahead, marking Greggs's and Islaen's progress.

There was no wavering, he thought as he watched the
slowing, moving glow that showed where Islaen was. They
had not linked thought very much, for each recognized the
other's difficulty and neither wanted to embarrass the other in
his misery. They did join occasionally, despite that reluctance, or he joined with her to offer what comfort and encour-
agement he could.

It was the least he could do, this small effort to ease her
way, if only in her mind. Whatever his discomfort, he knew
he was physically the stronger of them. If he were nigh to
exhausted and fighting to hold the pain of his straining muscles silent, the Noreenan woman had to be finding the crawl
many times worse, yet she gave no sign that she was having
any problem with it, either openly or in thought.

More time went by, a seeming eternity of grueling effort,
but at last Sogan imagined he saw a difference in the lights
pushing ahead of him. He closed his eyes and kept them shut
for several seconds. Weariness and anticipation might too
readily make liars of his senses.

When he opened them again and strove to see what lay
ahead, he knew that his first observation had been correct.
There was definitely a change. No longer did the two lights
reflect so brightly over so great an area. Most of the beams
must be going forward, out into some greater pit of darkness.

The light vanished, all but a faint glow.

His heart gave one painful jolt as a sensation of loss started
to rip him, but it faded quickly. Islaen and Greggs had merely
won free of the passage.

With the end of the ordeal before him, the Arcturian's
strength surged back, and he pressed forward with a speed he
had not been able to muster since entering the crawlway.
Soon a deeper darkness loomed before him. He could feel
Islaen just beyond his line of sight, and the lamplight showed
the floor of the new cave to be on a level with that of the one
through which he was crawling. He would neither have to

climb or negotiate a drop to reach it. He shoved his pack out before him and in another moment was free.

He lay sprawled where he was for an instant, trying to marshal the strength to force his cramped muscles to begin functioning again, then sat up. The world seemed to sway under him, but his consort's small, firm hand steadied him, and his senses soon settled.

Varn leaned against the cave wall, his eyes closed. He was ghastly tired, and the pain in his muscles was sharp enough to have wrung a moan from a less disciplined man, but none of that concerned him much. This was not the work he was accustomed to doing, but his body was hard. It would not be long in throwing off the effects of the crawl.

He looked around, taking careful note of his surroundings for the first time. They were in a cave, not large but quite high, thirty feet or more, he judged. The floor was rougher than they had encountered thus far.

The ubiquitous red stone was broken in three places by crevices large enough to allow passage by human body, that through which they had come and two others.

Islaen's gloved fingers brushed against his arm. *You're all right?*

He turned his face to her. *Why should I be otherwise?*

He smiled. *Aye, Colonel, especially since Greggs tells us there will be no more of this until the return.*

I'm not exactly crying about that myself, she agreed. *You were absolutely right, that's for sure.*

In what way? he asked in surprise.

Her eyes sparkled. *Anyone who engages in this sort of thing and calls it sport has to be raving mad.*

Her head snapped toward the entrance passage. Only a few minutes had elapsed since the Arcturian had emerged from it. Now an increased brightness told them that the remainder of their team was nearing the exit, and they readied themselves to give whatever aid they could.

Bethe came out first. She looked thoroughly spent and was patently glad of the support Islaen offered her.

Jake followed soon after. Varn was surprised to see how exhausted he appeared; illogically so, as if he had somehow expected the former Commando would not be affected by the ordeal at all.

He knew he looked no better himself—begrimed, sweaty, still a little white from his recent efforts—but for once he did not care. Let Jake take comfort from that if he would. He had earned the right.

Larnse Greggs stood back to watch the four off-worlders. The blue cast of his complexion seemed even more pronounced than usual, and he was glad enough to set his shoulder against the wall, letting it take some of his weight, but there was a cold kind of triumph in the smile he fixed on them.

"Well, how did you Federation space hounds enjoy your first encounter with Hades' underworld? No latent claustrophobia, I hope."

Islaen Connor whirled to face him, her eyes like a pair of angry stars. This was more than she could stand at the moment, or rather, more than she intended to let pass.

"That's quite enough, Greggs! None of us came to Persephone's system through any desire of ours. This is a serious assignment with potentially grave consequences for a lot of people, most particularly your own. I don't intend to complicate it with a petty revenge more in keeping with a nasty little child than a man. If this is an example of how you intend to conduct yourself, I'll terminate the mission right now and return to Horus."

"You wouldn't dare! Your orders—"

Her expression grew even colder. "I was given command when I received those orders, and with it the authority to carry out my mission as I judge best. My word, my decisions, will hold with respect to it. If I say we will not go after that planetbuster, then here it stays."

"Where it will remain a permanent threat not only to Hades, but to every other planet in the Sector," he reminded her.

"Not for long. Hades' space is already blockaded, and as soon as we have this hemisphere evacuated, we can bring in the armaments necessary to detonate the missile from the surface."

Her eyes bored into his. "Understand this, Larnse Greggs. I'm not merely an officer in the Federation Navy, but a representative of the Federation itself. In a situation such as this I have the power to do precisely what I have just said, and I will do it sooner than risk my comrades needlessly or expose them to the temper of an obviously hostile guide."

Her manner softened suddenly. "I know Hades had a hard fight, but so did we all in our own ways. You don't have to tell Jake or me anything about the difficulties and terrors of resistance work. We did it for four years as part of a penetration team on Thorne."

She glanced at the blond spacer. "Bethe, here, had an even worse job in the Demolitions Unit. She spent her time either setting Federation explosives or trying to disarm malfunctioning Arcturian missiles of one sort or another before they could wake up and go off in her face. Not a nice task at all, and I believe not many doing it regularly survived more than nine months or a year."

The Hadesi made no reply for several seconds, then glared at Sogan. "What about him?"

"Regular service. You may not have experienced war in space, but I've seen a little of it, more than enough to assure you that it's no joy." Her lips tightened. "The Federation owes more to his courage in terms of lives spared, innocent lives, than to all the rest of us put together."

Bethe Danlo took a step forward. "We're not responsible for the aid High Command could or couldn't, did or didn't, send you, Mr. Greggs, and we don't need you to like us, but we have to work together, for Karst's sake and the sake of a whole lot of other people who don't deserve to have to live in dread of being blown to atoms."

"She's right," Islaen said, picking up the argument from the spacer again. "No one's saying that most Hadesim haven't borne a great deal and deserve to be able to rest now, but there's another group amongst you who are, perhaps, entitled to even more."

"Another group?" he demanded.

"The children born since the War. They can run free, untouched by its blight. This shadow from the past mustn't rise up to sear them too. We can't let that happen."

His silence was different this time. "No. No, we can't," he said at last. He sighed. "I never intended treachery against any of you, and I'll lead you into no difficulty that can be avoided, either now or on the return. You have my word on that."

"Your word is assurance enough, Mr. Greggs.—What now?"

"Rest for a short while, eat a bit, and then go on."

The Hadesi moved away from them after that and sat down beside one of the unknown cracks in the cave wall, which they thus took to be their exit from it. He fumbled in his pack and took out a portion of his rations. The others followed suit.

Islaen stared at the wedge of high-energy concentrate in her hand but felt no hunger for it. She was too tired and dispirited to have much of an appetite. Larnse's transmissions, filled as they were with anger and mistrust, were unpleasant to receive, exhausting emotionally to endure long-term, but she would have to continue monitoring them. . . .

She looked up as a comforting warmth flowed into her. Varn had felt her inner weariness and was giving what he could of his own strength to counter it.

We need that man, Varn. One slip, any mishandling of this on my part, and we'll have to abort. The Hadesim were very careful about not giving us the actual route to the arsenal, even if we could negotiate the way without a guide.

You are doing well, he replied slowly. *A diplomat must sometimes act forcefully. I believe you had no other choice in this instance, and I believe as well that your strong stand has worked, at least to the point of improving the situation.*

I hope you're right, she said wearily.

You do not trust him?

We don't have to worry about treachery. I'm sure of him there, but that temper of his is another matter. I wouldn't put too much past him in the way of spur-of-the-moment violence if it went off at the wrong time.

That is why you and Jake have been mapping since we made our descent?

Her brows arched, but she answered him seriously. *We, or at least I, don't fear betrayal, not at Larnse Greggs's hands, but fortune's another thing entirely. An accident could deprive us of the only one who knows either the way ahead or the way out. We can't do much about the former, but both of us prefer to secure knowledge of our return route. —I didn't think we were so obvious about it.*

You are not. I was just hoping you would do so and was watching for it.

A smile brushed her lips. *Natural Commando nervousness is driving us. What's your excuse?*

Sogan glared at her for a moment, then allowed his humor to match hers. He should have realized that this woman would observe his jotting down the details of their position even more quickly than he had noticed her.

I cannot afford to share your trust in Greggs. He needs Bethe, and I believe he has a grudging but real respect for you and Jake, but he might have little trouble convincing himself to lose me in some maze if he could manage it conveniently.

His eyes dropped to the forgotten concentrate in her hand. *Eat that,* he ordered. *We will be moving soon, and there is no telling when we will be stopping again.*

Her eyes sparkled. *Aye, Admiral,* she agreed obediently.

An eager squawk welcomed her words, and Bandit's black-banded head appeared from beneath Islaen's jacket, emerging just above the second button from the top.

Varn gave a low laugh. "No one has to issue any commands to you when it comes to food," he told her.

Gurries are sensible.

You are the proving of that, small one.

He responded to her unspoken demand and lightly ran a gloved finger down her neck. *You are all right?* he asked.

Larnse had been correct in saying these caves were cold. His exertions had warmed him while they were in the crawl-way, and he had not been aware of the chill, but now he could feel its bite even through his heavy clothing. It must seem sharper still to the gurry.

Bandit's fine. My feathers keep me warm enough, but it's better inside jacket.

She said nothing more until she had finished the last of the rations Islaen had shared with her.

Good, she pronounced with real satisfaction and began a contented half whistle, half purr which ended abruptly a moment later. *Bandit doesn't like it here. Caves are dreary. Jade's nicer.*

No one's going to deny that, love, Islaen agreed, brushing off her hands.

We should be going soon, she told her companion. *Let's see what Jake and Bethe are up to. They'll think we're an odd pair if we go on much longer sitting here in seeming silence.*

Jake knows better.

Aye, but Bethe doesn't, and he's hardly going to enlighten her. Besides, we can't just close them out. Even if we didn't have to function as a team, I couldn't treat them that way.

No, I suppose you could not, he agreed, sighing in his own heart but rising readily enough to follow her.

TEN

Larnse Greggs soon called for the party to begin the next phase of their journey.

He leaned in the crevice they had already guessed would be their exit.

"You'll be seeing another side of Hades' underworld soon. You should welcome it and the fact that we won't have to work as hard for a while."

Islaen privately felt that, while she would indeed be glad of an easier course, nothing was very likely to alter the opinion she had already formed of these dank holes. But she was careful to give no indication of that as she followed the Hadesi.

The tunnel she entered was very narrow, so much so that she had to turn sideways at one point to pass through it, but it was short. A few minutes after stepping into it, she emerged again to find herself standing in yet another chamber.

She gazed at the world before her in open wonder. A chamber it was. If the caves and corridors she had seen thus far were cramped and bleak, not so this new one. This cavern was big, huge, although not quite large enough to completely defeat their powerful lamps. Hades' spirit seemed to have taken wing in the fashioning of it, for an incredible number and variety of speleothems, some of them showing delicate, extraordinarily beautiful variations in color, were visible on every side.

Great, conical stalactites and equally impressive stalagmites, their rounded counterparts, were to be seen on every side along with enormous numbers of slender and fragile soda straws. A number of columns had been formed where stalactites and stalagmites had actually grown together over the millennia.

Each of these last was circled by a large, flat protuberance four feet from its base, shelfstone deposited at a time when the cave had supported a lake. They marked its former level.

The cavern was still wet, and the signs of water and the effects wrought by it over great expanses of time were everywhere to be seen. Just above her hung a magnificent deposit of thin, rippling stone, or more precisely, calcite. The cave draperies, as she remembered such formations were called, were exquisite not only in the grace of their flowing shape, but in the fine striping of various intensities of red and orange marking them.

In several places on the wall beside her, she could see what appeared to be flowers. So they were in a sense, but flowers fashioned out of living stone, each petal having been pushed out into the cave as others formed in the porous rock behind it.

More common than these were the wildly twisting helictites, tiny tubes growing on walls, ceiling, and floor alike. They had been formed as the water forced up through their hollow centers capillary action deposited its minute mineral load at the ever-expanding tip, drop after drop, as previous slope and gravity dictated year after long year.

Perhaps the most significant feature of the chamber as far as they were concerned was the small river—a stream, really—flowing in a deep, steep-walled bed almost exactly through its center, until it vanished into a low place on the opposite side of the cave, nearly at the limit of their lamps' range.

"What do you think?" Larnse Greggs asked, speaking more softly than she had heard him do before.

"This is truly lovely," she responded without hesitation and with complete sincerity. "Everyone's read about the wonders some planets hold beneath their surfaces, but this is the first experience I've had with them. No reproduction or printed description can equal it."

"This system is a minor one. Hades has others that make where we are now plainer than that miserable crawlspace, but most of them are extremely hard to reach."

He smiled, a true one, about the first she had seen on him.

"I suppose, like all great beauty, it must be wooed and won. Rightly so, too, if it's to be appreciated as it should."

He was speaking like a lover, Islaen thought, but then, he was that—a lover who had striven mightily and long in his beloved's cause. It had been like this with the Thornens as well. She recalled the almost religious fervor, the depth of the passion, that had gripped so many of the captive planet's boldest fighters when they spoke of their homeworld even casually. It was only natural to assume that Hades' offspring would respond to her in her great need with equal devotion.

"Aye," she agreed. "It's always best that humankind should have to work for those things worth having, whether they be possessions or higher treasures like this."

The Commando gave a little sigh and seemed to straighten. "It's time to push on, I imagine?"

He looked down at the two hefty bundles he had manhandled through the crevice. "Now that I've brought these through the tight spots, I'd appreciate some help with them."

"You've got it."

"Good. —This'll be the easiest phase of the trip, mostly a ride, except for a few spots where we'll have to carry the boats. Luckily, there's good head room all the way, so we won't have any problems raising them."

"The boats are necessary?" Islaen asked. She liked the idea of the rest they would afford, but not at the price of taking on needless heavy labor.

He nodded. "We have to pass through another cave bigger than this one and go a little way into a second. The river almost completely fills the passages between each of them. It may not look like much, but it's too deep for wading, and it's cold. Why get wet before we must?"

"We will have to get wet?"

"Eventually."

"Well, let's be getting on with our boat building, Mr. Greggs."

It did not take long to carry the two bundles to the bank of the fast-moving stream, and scarcely more to transform them into slender, sturdy-looking little vessels. Of Hadesi design, they had been created for use underground. Although soft-sided and light, they were strong enough to withstand the challenges they could be expected to encounter.

Each was made to hold four people and their personal gear and could bear more in case of dire need, but they would not be asked to carry even their normal load during this mission.

"One would probably have done us," Larnse explained as they boarded, "but we'd have a hard time with the missile on the way back."

"I prefer having a second anyway," Islaen told him, "just in case of trouble."

She took her place in the stern and picked up the narrow paddle Greggs had put there. Sogan was already on board. He was in the center, between her and the guide, and would play no active role while they were on the water. Jake Karmikel and Bethe Danlo manned the second craft.

In another moment they had cast off. The current was strong, and there was little to do beyond keeping the boats away from the rough stone banks, but the guerrilla found plenty to occupy her in the wonder of the strange world around her.

They crouched down when they finally reached the end of the cave and the mighty stone walls closed in around the river. For several seconds walls and roof loomed chokingly near, as if they sought to meet, but then they withdrew abruptly again and the river hurried into a second cavern.

This chamber was much like the first, except that it was both narrower and considerably longer.

It was more rugged as well, Islaen soon realized. Boulders of every size could be seen lying amongst the speleothems, and it was necessary to watch for obstructions jutting out from the banks or up from the river bottom. Several times they had to come ashore and carry their vessels around such places, once for a distance of over one hundred yards.

Islaen worked with Jake and Bethe on these occasions, leaving Varn to help Greggs with the portage of the first boat. It was the most efficient way of distributing their strength, and although she greeted the ending of each episode with an inward sigh of relief, she felt it was to the party's good to force both men to work together.

The cavern narrowed steadily as the stream carried them toward its farther end, and when they passed through the exit tunnel and emerged again, they found themselves in a place that could nearly be named a true canyon. The cave walls loomed close, with only a ledge four to five feet deep on either side remaining of the banks. The roof had retreated and now soared so far above that their lamps were powerless to reach it.

A second, much smaller stream flowed downward from some source high above and joined with the first, adding just enough to its volume to make it a worthy little river.

The first boat had not quite reached their point of union when Larnse Greggs called a halt and signaled the off-worlders to disembark.

The site was an intriguing one, and all four studied it with considerable interest. The new stream flowed down through what looked like a series of seven steps, each in actuality a small pool enclosed by a lip of stone, a rimstone dam.

They were lovely to look at, but they gave Islaen a bad feeling, and she turned inquisitively to the Hadesi.

He read her question easily enough and nodded. "We climb them, the first five, at any rate." He paused. "After that we face the worst part of all this. It's bad, and it's dangerous. I hope you space hounds can handle it."

Jake frowned in annoyance. "A blindfolded man did, from what I understand of your history."

Greggs shook his head. "He wasn't blindfolded on that stretch. It would've been nothing less than murder to try to bring him across that way."

"He made it, though?"

"Of course. It's not impossible, merely tricky, with enough peril in it to warrant a warning."

"Let's get at it, then," the Noreenan man said grimly.

"As soon as we stow the boats. They have to be dismantled, stuffed in here between this bottom dam and the wall, and covered up with some of these rocks."

"You're expecting trouble?" Bethe asked sharply.

"The effect is that of hiding them," the guide admitted, "but it's just the usual procedure here. Flooding can occur at any time—it's one of the deadliest variables in caves like this—and we don't want to risk having them carried off."

Once that task was completed, the climb began. It was

harder work than it had seemed at first glance. The walls separating each dam were steep and high, and the constantly flowing water kept them slippery. That last added to their discomfort as well. Although not deep, it was numbingly cold, and there was no avoiding wading through it when moving from the edge of one dam to the base of the next.

Islaen Connor was breathing heavily as she fought her way up the face of the third obstacle. She reached the rim and hauled herself across it.

She stood there for a few seconds, bent over so that she might lean on it, before turning to face the next obstacle. Suddenly, she went to her knees, oblivious of the icy water.

"Larnse! Wait up!"

Greggs broke off his own climb. Muttering in annoyance, he turned back to help her. He saw at once that the Commando did not appear to be in trouble. She looked like she was examining something on the rim of that third dam.

"What's wrong, Colonel?"

"I'm not sure. Maybe plenty. Take a look."

He bent over the place to which she pointed, then straightened with a vicious oath, his pale eyes flashing. Chips, small but quite discernible, had been broken out of the delicate structure of the rim. No Hadesi had done that. It was the work of off-world footgear, probably a boot set with metal cleats.

The others had reached them by then.

Karmikel took one look at the damage. "How old is this?"

"Not very," Larnse answered. "I can't tell exactly. Two or three days, certainly nothing more recent, or our guards would've stopped them from coming down."

A chill filled his heart as he spoke. Any Hadesi who could bring an off-worlder into this cavern shod in that manner, knowing damage to Hades' ages-old beauty would inevitably result, must be brutalized or maddened almost beyond humanity itself. If his kinsman was indeed involved and had sunk to that. . . .

He drove those thoughts down.

"We can assume we have lost this portion of the race. We'll meet this other party on its way back from the arsenal. Exactly when will depend upon the kind of luck we both have."

ELEVEN

THE FIVE FINISHED the ascent of the next two dams. Starting from the base of the sixth was a foot-wide ledge which snaked its way upward and to the left at a steep angle. Greggs stepped onto this and, without speaking to the others, began moving up along it.

Islaen followed after him without any show of hesitation, slowing her pace and turning her body toward the wall as he did, to accommodate their more treacherous trail.

Up and up they went. After a while it seemed that the ascent would never stop, but when they had risen to what she judged to be approximately four hundred feet, the slope began leveling off. They followed it a short while longer, then their guide signaled a halt.

The Commando studied the way ahead of them, and the color drained from her face.

There before them was the sheer, utterly perpendicular wall of the great cave, one vast stretch, probably no more than seventy feet, though it seemed infinitely longer to her horrified eyes. Only this one ledge broke its face, if that pathetic line could be so termed. A few feet farther on it shrunk from the relatively comfortable support on which she stood to a thread that looked to be scarcely five inches across.

A line had been strung along the cliff at about chest height to an average Hadesi, but what real comfort, much less good, would that paltry support be?

Below—very far below—lay the ribbon of the river with its boulder-riddled banks, a somber, terrifying scene scarcely visible at the extreme end of her lamp's effective range.

A hand closed over hers, and Islaen looked up to find Larnse Greggs standing beside her.

"Look at it now. Satisfy your curiosity, then take your eyes off it and keep them off."

She nodded. "Sound advice."

"It's not all as bad as this part. The ledge widens by as much as a couple of inches along most of the route, but there's one spot, five feet of it, where it shrinks again and tilts down besides. It's right at the end. Watch for it, and take your time crossing it. We're in no hurry."

"I will." She gave him a tight smile. "Thanks, Mr. Greggs."

"For what? I don't like this either." He hesitated. "Look, Colonel, I don't want to start anything with Karmikel or Sogan, but they're both bigger men than any Hadesi. Are they going to be able to manage?"

"I'll put it to them—Greggs, why in the name of space didn't you tell us about this? Your warnings were no warnings at all."

"I know. I haven't come this route in years. It simply didn't fully connect until a few seconds ago, when I actually saw it again. Apologies are worthless—"

"Never mind, Mr. Greggs. I've made worse slips."

The Commando sighed in her own mind. His distress was real enough, but that was no comfort to any of them.

Varn, she asked, *Can you do it? It'll be awfully tight.*

I can try. What about Jake?

The redhead tersely agreed to make the attempt, then Islaen inched her way forward to the place where the ledge narrowed.

Terror closed her throat, all but choked her, as she started to move her foot onto the ledge. She stopped, momentarily frozen.

Easy, Islaen. Take it slowly and use the rope for support. You have a spacer's balance. Trust in that.

Sogan severed the contact then, fearing to distract her or draw any of her concentration from the task ahead of her.

She kept her body pressed against the cold, perpetually damp stone, taking as much support as she could win from it.

She slid onward with arms upraised and feet somewhat spread, giving herself four reasonably spaced points of contact with her support. The rope proved more helpful than she had originally imagined, for by thrusting her arms up through it, it served to hold her against the wall and made her feel less top heavy and likely to tip over, despite the weight of her pack. She marveled at the stark courage and determination of those who had stapled it to this place and those who came here periodically to see to its maintenance.

She longed for a safety line. Larnse was a careful man, a professional in subsurface ways and work, but the use of such devices had apparently never become established on Hades, and he had not thought—maybe had not even known—to propose adopting them here. She knew enough from her mountain training and was well enough equipped to rig something up, but it would not have sufficed. Any such line would have to be manually unfastened and moved over each of the staples, and she could not stand still in this place and fumble with it. She lacked the experience. She lacked the nerve.

On and on she crept, advancing scarcely an inch with each tense motion of her foot. Greggs was right. The ledge did widen a bit, enough to comfort her a little, although she doubted it would make much difference to either of her male comrades.

That easing of the way was only temporary. Islaen realized that, and her fear escalated with each second that passed, each step that brought her that much closer to the trial yet to come, the one Larnse Greggs had described before starting off himself.

She came to it at last. Her heart slammed painfully as she felt her ankles turn, her feet slip a very little.

Tears of pure terror rolled down her cheeks, but she kept moving onward. There was no other choice but to continue. To freeze was to fall, and to go back, with the other three already on the ledge, was even more impossible. She would only succeed in bringing them all down if she tried that.

A single sob of relief broke from her as first one foot and then the second straightened once more. The ledge widened perceptibly and rapidly under her, and a couple of minutes later a hand grasped her wrist, drawing her forward onto a broad, tablelike structure a comfortable twelve feet in width.

Greggs slipped a steadying arm around her shoulders. "You handled that like a master, Colonel. Here, catch your breath for a moment, then we'll get set to haul your friends in."

The mention of the others whipped the woman out of herself. She stood frozen as she watched them crawl across the stone wall, feeling sick in every fiber of her being. While making the attempt herself, her attention had been fixed on the one spot over which she was passing, one tiny position ever shifting into another, equally tiny. Now she could see the whole, the width of it, the awesome blackness above which no light they had could penetrate, the flow of the sheer wall down to its base in the murky darkness four hundred feet below.

Her eyes closed. The ledge that was their path and their sole safety looked so minute when laid against such an unforgiving expanse as to seem not to be there at all.

A cold, all-encompassing fear forced her eyes open again. Varn Tarl Sogan had reached the worst spot.

It was five feet long—only five feet, she told herself—but it had felt like that many miles to her.

Varn must make it! He had to make it. If he did not, if she saw him plunge to those rocks below, she would complete her mission if the Spirit ruling space and the gods of this planet allowed, but she would never again emerge as a living woman from Hades' underworld. That she vowed on her soul. His death would be her fault. She had permitted him to come here against her own judgment. She had allowed him to enter into this danger when her order would have kept him safe.

The Arcturian was across! She sprang forward, catching his hands as soon as he had reached the relative safety of the widening ledge and drawing him onto the haven the broad table provided.

He pressed her to him, holding her so tightly that the pressure of his arms was painful, for once openly asking comfort, sharing a terror as deep as her own had been.

That lasted but a moment. He stepped back after that, his

control fully in place once more, although he kept one arm around her.

Bethe Danlo was approaching the deadly crossing. Her small size had worked for her, and thus far she seemed to have had considerably less difficulty than either of the men. Her feet simply fit more securely on the tiny space available to support them.

She slowed significantly when the ledge turned down, as they all had, and continued on with ever-greater caution.

Suddenly her lead foot skidded as she put her weight on it. The spacer fought desperately to recall the step, to regain some measure of balance, and succeeded enough to momentarily break her fall, but it was painfully obvious that her respite was only a brief one.

Her fingers had curled around the rope as she went down, and it was by their tips that she now clung, her grasp weakening with each agonizing micro-instant that passed. All her weight was concentrated on her hands. Her legs were useless. The barest tip of one still pressed on the ledge but could not provide support, much less the leverage she needed to right herself. The other dangled helplessly against the unyielding wall.

The foot still in place started to slide.

Bethe Danlo moved. It was no wild, foredoomed scramble for purchase, but a leap. Drawing her legs in against her body, she thrust them against the cliff and sprang.

Breath, and even her heart, froze as she shot out and up. She moved her legs inward as she felt herself begin to start down. There was one chance, one slender chance. If she failed, she was lost. Her fingers would never bear the strain. . . .

Her feet struck the ledge and held, but only the the very edge. They could not retain their place, nor could she move to better her position without losing it entirely.

"Bethe, hang on! I'm with you!"

Jake Karmikel had started for her in the same moment he had seen her slip. Driving on at a speed that seemed a stark challenge to death itself, he was now at her side.

The former Commando wrapped one arm in the rope to hold himself in place. He leaned forward and caught hold of her, pressing her against the cliff and steadying her enough so that she was able to find her balance once more.

Varn Tarl Sogan had started to climb back out to her as well, but when Bethe stabilized herself and began moving again, he stopped where he was. When she reached him, he carefully linked his fingers with hers in a strong, reassuring clasp until he had guided her back to the safety of the stone table. That done, he returned again to perform the same service for Karmikel, realizing the redhead could be scarcely less severely shaken. Only when all the party was secure did he finally quit the narrow place and return to their haven once more.

TWELVE

BETHE DANLO LOOKED back along the way she had come. Thus far she had managed to hold firm and cold as Hades' own heartstone—anything less would have slain her—but now, seeing the doom she had so narrowly escaped, she began to shake, despite her effort to hold still before these others.

Jake was beside her in a moment, folding her in his arms. He was still white himself after that crossing, and he had endured nothing in comparison with her experience. He felt almost ashamed because of that, and he strove with all that was in him to give this valiant woman everything he could of comfort and human support until the reaction to her ordeal had passed.

The others left them alone. In truth, the former Admiral scarcely seemed to notice her trouble. He had been studying the narrow ledge himself, and questions had begun rising in his mind.

Until this point both he and Larnse had more or less ignored one another as far as was practicable, but now his cold eyes fixed on the Hadesi.

"Greggs, no one carried any planetbuster over that, whole or in pieces. Our packs were well nigh too much for us."

"No, of course they didn't. The party bringing it in split, half coming here, half remaining on the opposite side. They fixed a sling on a pulley and attached it to a rope suspended between them and sent the missile parts one by one. That's the way we'll have to manage it on the return."

"There's not much room for maneuvering over there," Islaen said slowly.

"We'll have to be careful," he admitted. "One of the women went over that other time."

"That's not happening to any of us," she declared firmly. "The first staple's close. I want whoever's over there hooked to it."

The on-worlder looked at her strangely. "I never considered that."

"No, safety lines aren't used on Hades, are they?"

"Not now, but they may well be after this."

"Thank you, Mr. Greggs. Some surplanetary folk label those wanting greater security than their own custom demands as cowards."

"Hadesim are a practical race, not a company of fools. Besides," he said, dropping his voice as he spoke, "after that woman's performance out there and the way your comrades went after her, I won't doubt either your skill or your courage again, whatever else I think of you."

Islaen nodded her acknowledgment of the compliment as she turned her attention back to the ledge. Her eyes ran the length of it, then focused on the place where Bethe had so very nearly toppled to her death.

"If only I could figure out some practical way of securing us during the crossing—"

She broke off with a softly muttered phrase in Noreen's ancient tongue. The spacer's Hadesi boots had never scarred the stone like that.

Varn's head snapped in her direction. Her actual, inner response to whatever had moved her was considerably sharper than the outlet she had permitted it.

Before he could question her with mind or voice, she had dropped, first to her knees, then to her stomach. Islaen squirmed right to the edge of the table and peered over it into the abyss below. Her light slowly swept back and forth across the broken ground beneath the titanic wall. It stopped moving.

"Train your lamps where mine's pointing," she ordered.

The others obeyed, each straining to make out what she had seen or thought she had seen.

In another moment they had spotted it. Distance and the twilight at the end of their beams made viewing difficult, but there was no doubting what lay there. It was a corpse, human or very like prototypical human, sprawled in a manner that indicated the spine had been shattered, not in one, but in several places.

Distance lenses told them more. The victim appeared to be male, although that was not entirely certain. His clothing was typical space garb. Its drab brown color made a poor contrast against the reddish stone and added to their difficulties in studying it. None of the five could make out anything in the way of real detail.

"Go down, Bandit," Varn Tarl Sogan ordered the gurry. "Search."

His mind touched hers. *Let me get a closer look at him. Go through any pockets or pouches you can reach. Make a show of that, as if we had trained you to do it.*

Bandit will do!

The little hen took wing and plunged over the edge even as she gave her answer.

Varn lurched forward as his sight receptors united with the gurry's, and he found himself staring at the ever-more-rapidly nearing cave floor, as if he himself were plummeting down through the air alongside the face of the cliff.

The Colonel caught hold of his arm. *Not yet, Bandit! Break contact. You're pulling him over!*

Jake was lying on the Arcturian's left. He felt him move, and turned in time to see Islaen grab for his arm. The redhead retained his Commando's reflexes. He might not comprehend what was going on, but he was quick to pin Sogan down on his own side.

In the next instant Varn's own eyes began feeding his receptors once more and his muscles relaxed. "Thanks," he whispered after a moment, keeping his voice low enough that only the two beside him could hear what he said. The others had been too engrossed in trying to follow the gurry's progress to notice his brief difficulty, and he did not want to draw any of their attention now.

Everything back to normal? the woman asked. She did not loosen her hold on him.

Aye.

"Look, you two," Karmikel hissed, speaking no more loudly than Sogan had before, "I can't mind talk, so what happened?"

"Bandit linked me to her eyes," the former Admiral explained. "The sensation of descent was so strong that for a moment my body started to follow her."

The other man whistled softly. "These talents of yours have their disadvantages, don't they?"

"Tell us about it," Islaen responded dryly. "Quiet now. We'll start attracting an audience."

There was little fear of that while Bandit remained a clear image in their companion's distance lenses, but once the tiny creature had descended to a point where the increasingly poor concentration of light interfered with their view of her, Larnse Greggs turned inquisitively to the Commando.

"You've really trained her to search a body?"

"Gurries are quite intelligent little things," she answered carefully. "The Navy and Patrol both use a variety of animals for a remarkable range of tasks. Her size limits her usefulness in a situation like this one, but she'll try to bring one or two documents back if she can find any she's able to lift."

"I was wondering why you kept her with you."

The Arcturian had been listening to their conversation. Now he turned to face Greggs. "We have her with us because we want her with us."

After that he forgot about the man again. Bandit had reached the cavern's floor and was asking him if he wanted her to reestablish the sight link between them.

Go ahead, small one.

He instinctively tensed as he once more began to see with the gurry's eyes, but there was no danger to him this time. The perspective was strange, as always, but there was little sensation of movement, and his two comrades kept their grip on his arms. He would not go over, whatever unexpected movement the hen might make.

Bandit flew slowly over the corpse, letting him get a good view of it.

The body was male, that of a very big man whose bulk was all bone and hard muscle, as had to be the case if he was what he seemed to be. Those who ranged the starlanes, particularly in rim Sectors, could rarely allow themselves the luxury of a soft, flabby body.

His size and what could be seen of his skin proclaimed him to be an off-worlder, as did his clothing. That was indeed typical spacer garb, all save the boots. They had not originated on Hades of Persephone, either, but were designed to give heavy surplanetary service rather than to be worn on the decks of a starship. The cleats studding their soles had probably caused his death, and they had left the marks on the stone ledge which had led Islaen to look below. Foolish things to wear here, he thought; it should have been obvious that they would give no purchase on stone.

There was no face, none that could now be studied. The head had struck hard when the poor devil had hit the ground, maybe struck it more than once if he had bounced, as his position indicated was very likely. If identification became necessary, it would have to be made from some other source.

The Arcturian had little interest in who the dead man had been, but knowing how long he had been lying there was another matter. That had considerable bearing on their own mission—particularly if they were wrong in their estimate of the amount of time the strange party had been in these caves already.

He needed to make a closer examination to determine that. He must at least have a better idea of the body's rigidity and temperature.

Land on him, small one.

As the hen swooped low to obey, he spotted movement around the corpse, on it.

Wait! Hold up, Bandit! Something else is down there.

She went in closer, almost touching the body.

He saw them, dozens of them. No, several hundred. Most of them were extremely small.

Beetles. They probably were not that at all, maybe not even insects, but the term was adequate at the moment for one with Sogan's limited knowledge of wildlife.

Although a few of them must have been a good inch in diameter, the vastly greater number were quite tiny. They ranged in shade from white to nearly transparent and were shaped like the circular metal coins common on most Federation worlds. They possessed five pairs of short legs, and their backs supported a fuzzy mop of what looked like antennae or tentacles and were probably a combination of both.

A moment's observation was sufficient to reveal what the creatures were doing.

Varn's eyes closed as he battled to keep his revulsion from forcing him to sever the contact.

Bandit was surprised by his reaction. *Bugs only scavengers. Jade has many too. They're needed, Varn.*

I know.

The man gripped himself. She was right, and this was not so monstrous a sight that he should play the coward because of it. The process was not nearly far enough advanced to so affect anyone accustomed to death. He had certainly seen worse.

They were not ravagers, either, though the mere sight of them congregated and scavenging brought vivid images of Visnu's living nightmare back into his mind. That marching, all-consuming hunger, or anything resembling it, would have devoured a food source like this in minutes, in seconds, not left it all but intact for hours or probably days.

Still he hesitated to let the gurry continue with her examination. How would those multifooted creatures react to the arrival of the tiny mammal in their midst. She might well be vulnerable to their preying. Their transmissions told him almost nothing. The intelligence level was too low to allow for emotion, at least of a kind he could receive, and he was able to detect little beyond the life spark and an abiding interest in the feasting in which they were engaged.

Islaen, do we go on? he asked the Commando after quickly filling her in on what he had observed thus far. She had decided against linking her receptors with his to share in the impressions Bandit sent him, chiefly as a precaution against the chance that some move or reaction of the gurry might threaten the balance of both; Jake would not be able to save the two of them. *You are the expert in this.*

Hardly that, she responded grimly, and retreated into her own inner mind for a few seconds. *Go ahead,* she decided at the end of that time. *They might attack her if she were injured, but an assault on a sound creature that much larger than themselves would probably be so energy-costly that I'd say natural selection has bred the impulse for it out of them long since. Just be careful. Things may have developed differently on Hades. We don't know enough about her wildlife to be certain.*

You heard her, Bandit. Go ahead. Get what documents you

can find as well and let me scan them, but if there's even the slightest possibility those beetles will try anything against you, come back to us at once. Do you understand?

Bandit understand. I don't want to be eaten.

The gurry gingerly settled on the shattered head and set to work with her supple toes to ferret out the information Sogan wanted, transmitting it to his mind's touch receptors even as her eyes delivered the data they received to him. That done, she went about the task of searching those pockets and belt pouches she could reach. The pack lay pinned beneath the body in such a fashion that she could not get into it at all.

There was little to be found, hardly surprising in view of the dead man's presumed profession. Pirates seldom carried much that might serve to identify them or betray their comrades. Varn went over it all quickly through the gurry's eyes. Only one piece looked as if it might be useful, a crewman's ID from a vessel called the *Sting Shark*. If that were genuine and not a forgery, it might provide a lead to the man's wolf pack and maybe even to the mother fleet itself.

Bring that one and come back up.

Bandit did right?

You did a fine job, under unpleasant circumstances and with the bond of secrecy on you. No one could have asked more of you, small one, and most might had expected far less.

THIRTEEN

A FEW MINUTES later the gurry was back amongst her human comrades, purring in the rapture that only one of her kind could display as they heaped praise on her. That of Islaen and Varn gave her the most joy, although they had to confine the full expression of it to their thought sendings. They knew what she had actually done and the role she had played while accomplishing it.

"You were wonderful, love," Islaen whispered as she started moving along the ledge once more in response to Larnse's signal. She opened her jacket again to admit the hen to her former perch. "Come and warm yourself now."

The Jadite creature whistled in contentment as she took her place. *Bandit's glad to be back,* she confided. *It wasn't nice down there.*

"I know. That's what makes what you did for us all the finer."

Her love for the gurry waxed greater still as she felt the tiny body snuggle in against hers. She was so small and delicate, and yet her courage and will to help were already proven.

Varn felt the swelling of tenderness in the woman and moved closer to her. *Still petting our feathered comrade Colonel?*

Of course.

Sometimes I wish I could come in for a share of all that attention.

Islaen saw his smile and matched her response to it. *No you don't, Admiral. You'll put up with only so much protection.*

Bandit's head slipped out from beneath the jacket and she gave a low whistle. *Bandit deserves attention.*

The Arcturian broke into the soundless, totally free laughter that never failed to surprise and delight Islaen.

"That you do, small one!"

The gurry's feathers ruffled, but merely for form's sake. She had long since learned how rare this response was for him and that she was the only one who could readily win it from him. She enjoyed her ability to do so, and it delighted her to be able to give him pleasure. Even more important to her was Islaen's grateful thanks.

The lightness soon left the humans' mood. Their mission was a serious one, and their discovery that others had penetrated the caves before them made it even more so.

You say the body appeared to be two to three days dead? Islaen asked.

So it seemed. That would coincide with Greggs' earlier estimate.

You have your doubts?

I do not know. What if it were here longer? Considerably longer? They got on-world before the blockade was set. They may have already taken the missile out and be well away again.

The woman's head lowered. *I don't think it's been here nearly so long. The cold might retard decomposition, right enough, but it wouldn't be in as good condition. Those beetles or whatever they are mightn't be fast workers, but judging by what you saw of them in action, they'd have gotten further if they'd had significantly more time.*

If he fell on the return?

A possibility, unfortunately, but I believe the intruders would've been picked up by the Hadesim guard or almost certainly stopped by the blockade on their way out of Persephone's system. Greggs kept dead quiet about his suspicions, much less about contacting us, and they'd have had no reason to expect an active watch against them. They'd have marched right into our arms.

Unless they were able to move before that watch was set, he pressed.

I've admitted the chance. They just might have made it out of the caves before the Hadesim arrived. In that case we'll find the arsenal empty—that'll be right bad for Hades. The Navy moved sooner than the locals, and they won't get by the blockade, but if they suspect it or somehow get back on-world with the planetbuster, and we can't take it in time, a lot of people are likely to die.

The Arcturian nodded. Pirates or their agents would not be permitted to bring that thing away with them, whatever the local cost. The ultimate result could be too many times more deadly.

We always seem to have that shadow over us, he said grimly.

He put that dark possibility away from him. There were more immediate concerns before them.

As you say, that is an outside chance. What is likely is that we shall probably be meeting with those others on their way back from the arsenal. Larnse Greggs is all too right about that.

Aye. I fear we can anticipate a battle at some point, she agreed.

How big a party will we be facing? Any ideas?

Islaen shrugged. *I'd say between five and ten. Fewer than that would have trouble managing the missile, much less of meeting any sort of emergency, and more would be both unwieldy and too likely to attract attention before or after their excursion underground. They're mostly all off-worlders, don't forget, and this jaunt had to take some preparation.*

The fact that they left no boats back at the dams makes me suspect the larger number, she added. *They were able to bring them along. We'd have been hard pressed to do that.*

Maybe they just concealed them.

She shook her head. *No. They weren't expecting trouble. They would've tucked them behind the first dam, the same as we did with ours. I checked with Greggs, and it is the only suitable spot. We'd have seen them there.*

It is battle for us, then, he said with a sigh. *Your Admiral Sithe showed his usual foresight in assigning a Commando to this task instead of a mere diplomat.*

Neither said anything more for several minutes as each retreated into his own thoughts.

Islaen glanced back over her shoulder. *If trouble comes, it won't be for a while yet, and there's no telling how long we'll*

*be able to continue walking abreast like this. Why not grab
the chance for a talk with Bethe? You've been itching for an
opportunity.*

The war prince stiffened, and she shook her head almost
imperceptibly. Varn Tarl Sogan's pride would not risk a
rebuff for something so trivial as the satisfying of his curiosity.

*I want you to feel her out, Varn. We can't be at all certain
how far Greggs' personal honor and his loyalty to Hades will
hold him in an actual fight, especially against one of his own.
We don't need any more wild cards. At least let's find out
whether she'll accept you this far or if she'll lock up entirely.*

*Indicating that she might regard me as a greater threat
than a pirate fleet with a planetbuster for a plaything?*

Islaen chose not to answer that directly. *I'll be monitoring
the first stages of your encounter.*

As you wish, Colonel.

Sogan dropped back until he was walking beside the demolitions expert.

Islaen fixed on the emotions the other woman emitted even
as her contact with Varn let her share in the surface portion of
their exchange. After a few seconds, she relaxed. Bethe
Danlo welcomed the former Admiral's company and his knowl-
edgeable interest in her field.

She had ceased all but the lightest surface probing by the
time Jake's approach pulled her attention entirely away from
the pair.

He matched his pace with hers. "Greetings, Colonel."

She welcomed him with a bright smile. "Going to join me
for a spell?"

"That was my intention. It's about the first chance we've
had for any kind of a gab since coming down into this
miserable hole." He stretched his long frame. "At least we
can stand up straight in this part of it."

He glanced for a moment at Larnse Greggs, who was
moving purposefully along the now broad ledge several yards
ahead of them.

"How long's he going to keep on going anyway? I don't
see myself as an inner-system fop, but it's been a long and
trying day."

Islaen laughed. "So it has, and I did broach the subject of
stopping. Greggs wants to push ahead for another couple of

miles. We'll be back in a real tunnel by then, and he claims there's a good chamber for our camp in there."

The former Commando nodded. He had no desire to sleep on any ledge, however wide, after their adventures this day, and he liked even less the idea of bedding down on their main trail with a party of probable pirates in these caves with them.

His companion knew him well enough to make a good guess at his thoughts. "Poor Jake," she said softly. "You wanted out of the military, and you've been dragged into every mission we've had since you retired except that Astarte business."

"I know," the redhead answered quietly. "I've been thinking a lot about that." He smiled. "Maybe I shouldn't complain. The life seems to be doing well by you and the Admiral. And Bandit, of course," he added as he reached out and stroked her in response to her demanding whistle.

Islaen's eyes sparkled. "What happened back there? Did Varn put the run on you?"

"Not exactly. He and Bethe were so deeply engrossed in a discussion of a planetbuster's viscera that they forgot me completely, so I decided to nip up here to say hello."

"Good choice. I don't like being ignored, either."

"No chance of that, lass!"

Islaen smiled, but then more somber thoughts returned to her. "I'm glad she responded this way," she said gravely.

"Instead of treating your Admiral like a security risk?"

"Aye. She did suspect him at first."

"Oh, Bethe doesn't suspect anything, Colonel. She knows."

Her head snapped toward him. "What?"

"Admiral Sithe apparently neglected to mention that she had been in the honor guard at the surrender. She knows a member of the Arcturian warrior caste when she sees one."

Islaen Connor's eyes closed. "By Noreen's gods," she whispered.

"Relax. Bethe Danlo won't betray him. She considers his recent history more than vindication enough."

Relief swept through the Colonel. "She's holding to that or I've totally lost my ability to interpret transmissions."

"Of course she is! She said she'd stand as his friend, and I fully believe she meant and means just that.—Bethe's incredible, Islaen. How the Commandos ever failed to gra her, I'll never understand. Did you see that leap she made today?"

"The Commandos most likely failed to grab her because the Regulars knew what they had and wouldn't let her go," Islaen replied tartly. "As for the rest, aye, I saw what she did, and I never want to see anything like it again."

She shuddered. "I thought both of you were dead when you went after her the way you did."

"Ah, she needed help. Sogan got back on the ledge fast enough himself, I noticed."

"I was aware of that too."

The spacer shrugged. "Best forget it all for now. We'll just have to be more careful on the return."

"That we will," she declared tightly.

Islaen was quiet for a while. A frown started to darken her features, and her companion gave her a sharp look.

"Trouble?"

She quickly recalled herself. "No. I've been scanning, but no one's near."

"What's wrong, then? Something's biting you."

"Our two friends back there aren't Commandos. They're so involved in their discussion that they're completely oblivious to what's happening—or could happen—around them. Varn's depending on my talent to warn us of any danger, which, in principle, isn't very bright, and Bethe . . ."

"She's not thinking about danger at all. As you say, you have to be a guerrilla to constantly think like one. Right now the roof could cave in, and neither of them would probably notice."

"That's an unfortunate choice of phrase, friend, considering our present location," she remarked.

"But not totally inaccurate. There's no point in making an issue out of it, not at this stage, with the real chance of trouble so slight. I'll just drop back and cover our rear."

"Thanks, Jake. Only—"

"I know. I'll be very unobtrusive about it and not damage any tender egos." His blue eyes shadowed. "Bethe would not like to think she'd slipped on her part, either."

He left her with that. Islaen smiled and shook her head, but then her expression darkened. His remark about falling roofs kept pricking at her. She did not fear a total cave-in, she decided almost at once. It really was not likely, and besides, her concern felt more concrete than that. She tried to place its source. . . .

The unease remained with her even after the ledge ended, flowing into a true tunnel once more. It abated for a while, lulled by the sense of security afforded by having walls all around them, but it soon returned, redoubled in force.

The Commando's eyes narrowed as the answer surfaced at last. She knew what had been troubling her now, and she did not like it at all.

It was the increasing roughness of the caves through which they passed, the ever-growing number of boulders and piles of loose stone cluttering the otherwise smooth floors. They must have fallen from someplace.

It had not been a source of concern in those first caverns. The debris there had shown the softening effects of water, indicating most or all of the stuff had probably been carried in by long forgotten floods and set down in the distant past, but that was not the case in this tunnel. Rock lay on the floor, great slabs of it rather than rounded boulders, and open wounds remained in the roof above to show all too clearly from where it had come. There was not a great deal of such material, but there was more than enough to prick at her nerves and at the warning senses long years of deadliest form of warfare had honed to almost superhuman keenness.

Islaen quickened her pace and caught up to Larnse Greggs. "I have a question or two, Mr. Greggs."

He moved aside to allow her to join him. It was still possible to walk abreast, although no longer entirely comfortable to do so.

"If I can answer them, I will. What's the problem?"

"Most of the rock lying about here came from above. What are the chances of more falling?"

"In theory, ever present, I suppose, but in actuality, we have very little to worry about. All these falls are very old, most of them prediscovery.

"This tunnel and those leading from it are the most ancient we've yet found and are approaching the end of their life cycles. The falls are what we call cave breakdown since they are part of the process that will eventually fill the tunnel in. That wouldn't happen in our own lifetime, however, or in many lifetimes to come," he hastened to assure her, "even if we'd left nature alone to follow her own course."

"Which you didn't?"

Larnse shook his head. "We couldn't risk possible reper-cussions to the city above, so we imported sealants and strengthened the weaker places. We planned to do it all, but the War intervened. Most of the work was complete by then, though, and we'll be finishing up the rest in another year or so, once the major surface repairs are out of the way."

She thanked him and dropped back once more, considera-bly, although not completely, relieved.

Varn had broken off his conversation with the demolitions expert and moved up into his usual place behind the Colonel. She gave him a quick report of what had passed between her and the Hadesi and then fell silent. Both of them were tired, and although they kept their minds linked, neither felt like real conversation.

The party continued in this fashion for the next quarter mile. Several times they passed crevices in the walls, some of them looking as if they led to more cave.

Greggs stopped at one particularly large opening and waited for Islaen. "If you want to call a halt, there's room enough in any of these chambers for a camp, but I'd like to go a bit farther. Only this one has another way out, and we couldn't exit that way with any kind of speed."

"We'll continue," the Commando answered without hesi-tation. "Those pirates have an ex-Resistance man with them, and I don't want to take any chances of being trapped, not while we've got a better option."

"Thanks, Colonel. I was hoping you'd see it that way."

Less than ten minutes later they were brought to a halt. The tunnel was completely choked by a massive and apparently very recent rockfall.

Sogan studied the towering mound of rubble. There would be no passing it. The stuff rose right to the ceiling, so that even the place from which it had dropped could not be seen.

He turned to Larnse. "It seems you were wrong about the roof, Greggs—or perhaps you merely misjudged when it would go."

"If I'd wanted to get you that way, I wouldn't have

botched it!'' the Hadesi snarled. "We took out a lot of Arcturians like that in the early days, before we put the fear of the underground on them."

"All right, you two!" Islaen snapped. "That's not going to help us."

Her mind slammed into Varn's. *What in space is the matter with you? Stop antagonizing him.*

I have said before that I do not share your trust in him.

He's just as dismayed as the rest of us, and is highly embarrassed besides. Now lay off him!

Islaen seemed to be studying the rockfall as she spoke with Varn. Now she focused all her attention on it.

"When did it happen?" she asked. "Can you make a guess, Greggs?"

"Within twenty-fours hours. Probably far less than that." He picked up a stone splinter lying near his feet and held it up for her to examine. "See where it broke. The damp hasn't even darkened the new surface yet."

"Let's take a good look at that pile. I want to see if there's any indication that nature might have had a little help in bringing all that mess down."

A careful search revealed nothing untoward. "Well," she said at its end, "if we can't completely discount the possibility of conscious agency in this, I think we're safe enough in acting on the premise that it was the result of natural forces."

"That places the other party behind it," Sogan said.

"Aye, and presumably they're ignorant of it. The question is what they'll do when they find out. Mr. Greggs?"

"They have more or less the same options we do. They can try to dig or blast their way out, depending on how they're equipped, trusting that the fall isn't too deep and hoping their efforts don't bring more of the roof down on them, or they can forget about the planetbuster and come out by another route."

"You've mentioned alternate ways before. Where are they and what are they like?"

"At this point there's only one, although farther out a number of approaches lead into it. The way is tricky, hard in places, and there are a couple of very tight stretches that completely preclude the removal of a planetbuster."

"Could they be opened up with explosives?" the former Admiral asked.

Larnse looked at him with the distaste any son of Hades would display at that suggestion, but he answered evenly and readily. "One spot, maybe, although personally, I believe the attempt would be a failure. The second, no. It's too large. Besides, they wouldn't have the wherewithal with them."

"But we could go in that way ourselves?" Islaen demanded.

"Aye, or we should. There is risk."

"What do we do to get there?"

"Just backtrack a bit. The entrance is in that cave I mentioned as being the only one with a back door along that stretch of tunnel."

"How long will it take once we start?" she asked wearily. It would be difficult to begin anew after having already gone through so much.

"Assuming nothing's happened to the rope, and allowing for delays, two full days and some part of a third."

The Colonel's energy returned in a flash. "Then we might still be able to surprise them in the arsenal, or maybe even beat them to it?"

He nodded. "Possibly, if luck's with us and against them."

"You mentioned a rope," Jake interjected.

"It's a permanent fixture, like the one on the ledge. They wouldn't have had any reason to touch it, but you can never tell."

"We have rope with us," Bethe pointed out, "quite a lot of it."

"Not that much."

"This is beginning to sound unappealing," she whispered to Karmikel as the Hadesi turned his attention back to the Colonel.

Islaen seemed to be looking into the distance, but she was quick to recall herself. "If it isn't there or has been sabotaged?"

"We can still get to the arsenal, but it'll take a lot more time."

"Then let us hope it is in place and sound," Varn Tarl Sogan said. "We would do well to reach the missile before they do, or at least before they can go to work on it."

"What do you mean?" Greggs demanded sharply. The tone of Sogan's voice had sent a chill through him.

"I was talking with Bethe earlier. That vermin must dismantle the planetbuster if they are to remove it, the same as we must, but according to her, it is no simple task."

The blond spacer nodded. "The design for that missile class was changed drastically early in the War. Those old ones were basically fairly unstable, and anyone not specifically trained to manage them who starts messing about with one may be in very big trouble. No pirate demo man is going to have had that instruction. Very few even in my Unit did."

She frowned. "There's danger enough in the possibility of inexperienced hands creating havoc with it that I'd suggest making off with the heart of it, even if we must leave the rest. Without that, the bulk of it won't be a threat to anyone even if there's a major delay before it can be removed."

"I already told you we can't bring it away with us." Greggs said in exasperation.

Bethe Danlo smiled. "And I told you that planetbuster is obsolete. No parts have been made for it in decades. If I can actually go into it, as opposed to merely taking it apart in assembly sections, and remove two rods from it, each an eight of an inch by twelve inches, the rest is nothing more than a hunk of debris."

She grimaced and glanced at Islaen Connor. "It's not a job I'd normally tackle. One slip, and none of us'll make another.—What about it, Colonel? Do I go ahead with that part of it?"

"We'll have to see how it goes when we get there," the Noreenan told her grimly, "but you're the expert in this. I'm not likely to interfere with your decisions if circumstances permit you to make the try."

FOURTEEN

THE SMALL COMPANY was not long in returning to the crevice Larnse named as the pathway to their alternate route.

Inside was a large, roughly rectangular chamber at least thirty feet long and eleven wide. Better than a third of the floor on the innermost side had been swallowed by a gaping pit. A strong-looking frame of the same nonoxidizing alloy used for the staples on the ledge had been set up over it, and a veritable mountain of slender caver's rope was neatly coiled on the ground beside it.

Bethe eyed the last with no feeling of pleasure. "Just how much rope is there, Mr. Greggs?"

He grinned, reading her misgivings easily enough. "Thirteen hundred twenty-four feet, plus a few odd inches."

"I knew this was a bad idea," she muttered to Jake, who nodded glumly in agreement.

The Hadesi looked to Islaen. "It's your choice, Colonel, but it'll take time to check all this out and get set up, and even more for the descent. We're all bone tired, and since it's well nigh certain that we'll have no visitors to worry about, I think it'd be best all around if we posted a guard and bedded down here for the night."

She pondered that for only a few seconds. "You're right. We'll be better off starting out fresh. We'll eat and then turn in.— Bethe, you have the first watch, then Jake, Varnt, and myself. Mr. Greggs, you take the last stretch. You can use some of that time to start whatever preparations you have to make."

To her surprise the guide shook his head. He scowled at

Sogan. "I know very well that you don't entirely trust me.
Arrange it so that one of you watches with me."

Islaen nodded. "A good suggestion. That way you can
start your inspection of the gear without having to worry
about anything else. I'll watch with you."

The five wasted no more time in dropping their packs and
breaking out a larger portion of their supplies than they had
taken at their first break hours earlier. These they warmed on
Islaen's plutonium disk, then separated into the same groups
as they had on the previous occasion.

Weariness gripped them all, so that no one was eager for
the food, despite their exertions and the length of time since
they had last eaten. Even Bandit went at her share with less
than her customary eagerness.

She stopped eating after she had consumed about half her
share, and looked up into Islaen's face. *Should Bandit eat
less?*

"Why, love?" Islaen asked in surprise.

We have only the food we carry.

Varn, too, was taken aback. He broke off a piece from his
own portion and placed it in front of her. "These are called
rations, small one, but we are not rationing. Even if we were,
the little you take would not even affect our supply. Go ahead
and enjoy yourself."

He smiled at the rush of relief his assurance sparked in the
gurry, and touched his mind with that of his consort. *If only
we humans could be satisfied so readily.*

You and I would have to find some other line of work.

He stroked the small head, then withdrew his hand again.
What are these gurries, Islaen?

*I don't know. I've been wracking my brain about that ever
since she came to us, wondering if we have any right to keep
her with us even if it is by her own wish and will.*

Bandit gave an alarmed squawk and her feathers started to
extend. *Bandit stays!*

"Gently, love. We won't send you away. We just worry
about you now and then. We worry about each other, too,
you know."

Yes.

Once more, Islaen's mind opened into Sogan's. *For all
practical purposes they were animals before humans planeted*

on Jade, eating, mating, migrating with the goldbeasts, avoiding predators. Once they started dealing with us, things changed. They began facing intangibles, complex choices, and they rose to the challenge. What they are now—

The Jadite creature's thought broke into hers. *Bandit's a gurry!*

Islaen smiled. *I suppose that is the only real answer we have. Bandit's a gurry, and gurries are themselves.*

She opened her jacket to admit the little hen, who had finished the last of her meal by then, and moved nearer to the Arcturian. She settled against him as he slipped his arm around her to draw her close. She was tired, and it was good to feel the warmth and strength of his body against hers. She needed that sometimes, even with the greater glory they shared in the union of their minds.

Larnse Greggs watched the former Admiral without seeming to do so.

The look he bent on him was not friendly. Sogan should never have been permitted on-world in the first place and certainly should never have been allowed to stay so long. Under normal circumstances he would not have been, not even with his Navy rank and Commando affiliation to back him, but the relative urgency of this mission demanded some compromise. Old hate could not be permitted to bring preventable suffering and slaughter on innocent populations.

His pale eyes shadowed. The man was a mystery, too much of a mystery. He was so like their enemies, not only in appearance, but occasionally in his manner as well, that it seemed at times that the old days of terror were once more upon Hades; yet in other ways he seemed something totally different.

There could be no doubting his affection for that strange little Jadite animal, or mistaking the tenderness he displayed toward her—and as Bethe Danlo had pointed out, that was not the custom with Arcturians. That race of conquerors never concerned themselves with the lesser creatures of any world.

Then, too, there was his relationship with the Colonel. The warriors of the Empire maintained their women as playthings, decorations housed in their harems, not as battle comrades, much less commanders.

The Hadesi stopped himself there. This was one aspect of the invaders' lives about which he knew well nigh nothing as real fact. They were human, and so he supposed some sort of affection and even respect of a kind must occasionally rise between a man and his consort or one of his concubines, but something of this nature? That he could not believe.

He saw the auburn-haired woman rest against Sogan, cradled by his arm, and anger flared in him.

How could she permit it? She was a daughter of the Federation. More than that, she had actually fought the Arcturian Empire and had seen the agony of free people caught in its grasp. She had led the war of one such race. Even if this man were only a space mongrel or the son of one of the many planets giving rise to races with these physical characteristics, how could she stand to have him in her presence at all, much less wed with him and lay with him? Such was Varnt Sogan's resemblance to their enemies that her stomach should rightly twist at the very sight of him.

How had he managed it? What had that arrogant, cold-blooded bastard done to sway her to his will?

Islaen stiffened as the Hadesi's anger struck her mind. What in all space could have set it off?

The gurry hen slipped out of her warm nest. *Don't worry, Islaen. Bandit fix.*

She took wing and went to the on-worlder. His ill feeling faded under the combined pressure of amazement and Bandit's more subtle influence as the tiny creature perched on his knee and looked up at him, whistling in the manner he recognized by then as a demand for attention.

Larnse smiled as his self-conscious stroking elicited a storm of purring.

"You really do like that, don't you?" He looked from her to the two he believed to be her owners. "These gurries are nice little things. Any chance Jade will start exporting them?"

Islaen Connor shook her head. "The settlers feel they have resources in plenty without that, and they're concerned, with cause, given humanity's history, that they might suffer abuse or exploitation if they were allowed off-world."

"What about this one, then?"

"Bandit's the only exception."

The Hadesi frowned, and the gurry increased the power of her transmission in an only partly successful attempt to counter this new surge of hostility.

"They couldn't refuse Federation brass, I suppose."

Bethe Danlo's eyes flashed angrily. She had been lounging against the wall, using her pack for a cushion, but now sat bolt upright. "No way! Why don't you try getting a few facts before shooting off your mouth?—Colonel Connor and Captain Sogan were allowed to take the gurry because those people knew they could be trusted, and because it was a little hard to refuse them after they'd saved the whole damn colony and everyone in it, not once but twice."

"A real pair of heroes?" he asked, curious despite himself.

"That's right. They have three heroism citations, first class, earned since the War ended, two of them for what they did for those Amonites. Jake won a brace of them, too, for his part in those crises," she added proudly.

Her slate eyes bore into Greggs. "You may not like their choice, but the Navy sent Hades some pretty first-rate people."

Islaen, Varn, and Larnse soon settled down, wrapped in the warm, lightweight, spider-silk blankets that were standard issue for any such excursion, military or civilian alike.

Jake pulled his around his shoulders but did not compose himself for sleep. He moved over to the cave's mouth, where Bethe had already established herself for her stint on watch.

"Better wrap up," he advised. "Hypothermia's a real risk down here when one's not moving around, and it can be sneaky about the way it strikes."

The spacer complied. "That feels a lot better, but I was afraid I might doze off if I got too comfortable."

He shook his head. "I don't think so. Not you. Our day wasn't that strenuous anyway, and this is the first turn. Later ones are harder."

Her eyes twinkled. "I'm not sure how I should take that."

"As a compliment. You've been nothing but an asset so far." His tone grew even more serious. "Thanks for your defense before."

Bethe shrugged. "Space hounds have to stick together, especially Navy people."

"We're not Navy anymore," Karmikel pointed out.

Her brows lifted. "You think not?"

The woman watched him for a few moments. Her eyes wandered to where the Colonel and her consort were lying and then returned to Jake.

"Why did you let him take her?" she asked bluntly.

The Noreenan stiffened. "What do you mean?"

"I'd have to have my head in a black hole to miss the way you look at her."

He scowled, but decided to answer her, since he had been fool enough to betray himself. "I didn't let him take her," he replied sourly. "I was never in the running, not even when we believed him to be dead."

Bethe was quiet only an instant. "So you lose out on one charter, and now you refuse to ship any other?"

"What other?" he demanded irritably.

"Look, friend, when I planet, I like to get to know a bit about the world in question and her people, instead of swilling in the nearest port tavern, and we've had quite a few charters for Jade. It seems to me even from my surface-level explorations that more than one of those Amonite women would gladly trade her traditional isolation from other peoples and her planet-bound security to range the starlanes with you."

The redhead grinned despite himself, but he shook his head. "None of them would be happy in that life for long."

He eyed her. "Enough about me, Bethe Danlo. Now that you've opened this path, I'd like to know a bit more about you."

"Such as?"

"Your history."

"It's nothing worth recounting."

"I'm a great listener. Besides, I want to know how you latched into the Demolitions Unit. People might've been hammering the hatches to join the Commandos, but not your club. It was strictly a voluntary assignment, and I understand its ranks were never anything like full."

She smiled faintly. "I didn't seek out the job, I assure you. It came to me more or less by accident."

Bethe sighed as her memories of other times arose. "My father, three brothers, and I were crew and joint owners of a tidy little freighter, and in the manner of most of our kind, we ignored the War as best we could, confining our service to keeping the trade going if not entirely flourishing, among the planets in the Sector where we operated . . . passing on any odd bits of information that came our way, and the like.

"Then our Sector was hit. It was the last real conquest surge the Arcturians made, well after the general retreat had begun, but it was as efficiently and successfully conducted as any of their earlier efforts. More than half the worlds there were swept up. A number of them were well-known to us, planets where we had friends, some of them close friends, and my menfolk felt the need to take a more active role in their cause. They enlisted, leaving me to manage the *Jewel* as best I could since I was still really only a child at the time, far too young for the military even to consider accepting. Anyway, someone did have to stay with the ship."

Her head lowered. "Spacers are a stubborn lot, and my lads were no different. They insisted on being posted on the same ship, a practice the Navy does permit but strongly discourages, especially with members of an immediate family. They were on the *Terra's Pride* when she was blown, barely three months after they qualified for active duty."

She was quiet a moment. "I hired the services of a young spacer who had been left without a berth in the cutbacks forced on all the freighters following the invasion. Times were hard for us space hounds throughout the untouched portion of the Sector. Charters were few with so many of our customer planets captive or behind active battle lines, and those cargoes still being shipped were dangerous in the extreme to carry since the starlanes were filled with Arcturian ships of every conceivable class. Making a delivery amounted quite simply to blockade running.

"All the same, Norm and I managed to get by during the next three years, even if our belts were drawn pretty tight at times. We were even beginning to think in terms of a future for ourselves, when I was hit with a mild case of Quandon Fever. Norm took the *Jewel* up himself."

Her mouth twisted. "One person, and not even the ultrasystem's best pilot, trying to manage a five-man ship by himself, without anyone even to handle the weapons for him . . . but we needed the credits real bad just then."

Her voice wavered, but she steadied it. "The wreckage was discovered two days later."

"I'm sorry," Jake said softly.

Bethe smiled in gratitude. "Thanks, friend. —Anyway, there I was, no ship, no kin, and no prospect of work with most of the captains still flying not even able to keep on all of their old hands, so when I got back on my feet, I decided to enlist. I was old enough by then to be taken, and I was right in guessing that my space skills were sufficient to arouse some real interest.

"While I was awaiting transport to Basic camp, Arcturians struck our staging area. I made it to a shelter with five others, but we were scarcely inside before it suffered a direct hit. My companions were killed outright and I was knocked senseless.

"When I came around, I found myself looking at a long, scarlet-and-black missile."

"A death fury!"

She nodded. "It had been quiet, but even as I watched, it quivered, not much, but enough to show it was anything but a dud. It soon began shaking fairly steadily. There was no getting out—the exit was completely blocked—and from the way the fury was vibrating, I figured I had maybe fifteen or twenty minutes before it went off, so I thought I might as well have a go at disarming it. I'd always been interested in how things work, and I'd done a good bit of reading on weaponry over the years. I knew the Arcturians' and the Federation's both worked on the same basic principles, and I had at least a fighting chance. At the very least, doing something for myself was better than just sitting back in defeat and waiting to be blown to bits. Needless to say, I succeeded."

She giggled, and the shadow of the hard years gone by was stripped away. "A rescue team broke in to me just as I finished. You should've seen the look on their faces! They bolted out of there faster than the death fury had come in!"

Bethe grew serious once more. "One of them took enough note of the incident, despite the chaos following the attack, to report it. I found myself in the office of the Demolitions Unit's Sector CO before another day had passed. I suppose I was drunk with my success, and as I said before, I was truly interested in such things. When he described his Unit's work and the training I'd receive if I joined, I accepted.

"I was kept busy after that. The Empire's war machine was crumbling. Their forces, spaceborne or surplanetary, couldn't get the matériel they needed, and they were throwing everything they had left at us, even damaged and only marginally operable missiles. However, the War ended before I could slip and turn myself into so much space dust.

"There wasn't much need for our particular skills once peace came, and nearly the entire Unit was demobilized. Prospects were bleak for me in my old haunts, so I came out to the rim. Things didn't prove much more promising at first, but then fortune threw a smile in my direction. I ran into one of my father's old friends, the master of a freighter in need of a hand."

She colored. "I'll admit I played on that friendship to secure the place, but I've given him cause in plenty to be glad he took me on."

Her chin lifted. "I'll tell you right now, though, I don't intend to spend the rest of my life working my fins off on someone else's ship. There's been a Danlo on the bridge of a spaceship or starship since Terrans first took to space commercially, and I have no intention of letting that tradition die.

"I'm stashing away every credit I can lay my hands on, and when I have enough, I'll get a derelict or near-derelict, restore her, and head for the extreme rim. Maybe I'll never have what we had before our Sector was invaded, but she'll be my own, and a small freighter can do as well as, and sometimes better than, bigger ones right at the very edge."

"I wish you luck, Bethe Danlo. You've charted no easy course for yourself."

She shrugged. "It's little different from what you've begun doing with your *Moon.*"

"Aye, but sometimes the sheer magnitude of the task is all but overwhelming. Even with the credits from two class-one citations, I haven't been able to do a fraction of what I want."

"You'll manage, my friend.—Now go off to sleep, Jake Karmikel," she said sternly. "You need the rest, and I need to keep watch, which I'll never do properly if you stay here as a living temptation to draw me away from it."

FIFTEEN

A GENTLE TOUCH and an even softer caress in his mind recalled Varn Tarl Sogan to the chill, harsh world of Hades' underground. He started to sit up but lay still again, barely stifling the gasp of pain the sudden movement had surprised from him.

Instantly, Islaen's mind opened into his. *Varn, are you all right? Is the damp getting to your back? We haven't been faced with anything like this since Visnu.*

He sat up and worked his shoulders experimentally. *I am fine. There are a few twinges, nothing more. Your physicians performed a near miracle.*

I wish they could've fixed you up completely.

They did more than should have been possible with scar tissue so long established.

The Arcturian glanced about the chamber, looking for the others. Larnse Greggs was up, of course, since he had shared the final watch with Islaen. Bethe and Jake were just rousing themselves. Bandit was riding Islaen's shoulder, apparently in great form.

Varn watched the Hadesi man somberly. Islaen had told him about the seemingly groundless souring of his mood last night, although she had not joined her receptors with his since it had vanished again so quickly.

How did you manage with Greggs this morning?

Fine.

Her head lowered. She was busy repacking her gear after the night, and so could safely continue their conversation without calling attention to them because of their apparent silence.

104

Her monosyllabic answer made him fear there had been trouble, and his next query came more insistently. *Islaen, what happened between you?*

She favored him with a tight smile. *Nothing, Varn. He was civil, indeed as close to friendly as I've seen.*

Her eyes dropped back to her pack and the work she was doing. *He's got me worried. I don't deny that. His dislike of us remains, even if respect is beginning to war with it a little, and the conflict can't be helping his temper, which seems to feed on itself in any case. I greatly fear we'll have a major flare-up from him before the end of this, whatever we do. We came close to it last night, I think, and I don't even have an idea what set him off.*

Concern tightened both her thoughts and her expression. *Bandit saved the situation then, and she's been doing a hero's job in keeping him cooled down, but she can only induce good feeling, not control him. Even yesterday, it was more the surprise of her coming to him than her actual influence that shorted out his anger. If he actually lets go, she'll be powerless.*

Islaen closed the pack and began a final examination of her seat harness and fastening clip. There could be no chance that either would fail her on the way down.

We'll just have to play it carefully, I guess, and hope for the best.

She got to her feet and glanced at the others. There was no point in fretting over potential problems, not with work to be done and a concrete challenge before them.

Greggs and I have eaten already. We'll finish setting up the gear while you three are breakfasting.

She assumed a mock-stern expression as the gurry deftly transferred herself to Sogan's shoulder.

Go easy with the handouts. She's eaten already, too, and managed to charm another half-ration out of our guide.

Bandit was just helping! the gurry explained indignantly.

"Yourself and us," she responded dryly. "Oh, go ahead. You know you'd probably ruin Varn's morning if you didn't let him spoil you."

It would soon be ruined anyway, the former Admiral thought glumly as he eyed the big coil of rope, but he managed to shield his misgivings sufficiently to avoid having them enter into his consort's awareness.

His reluctance was more inspired by his desire not to add further burdens to her current load than any need for concealment. Fear was part of a warrior's life, and the unease he felt about this phase of their mission was no more than any of them must be experiencing, at least any of the off-worlders. He could not imagine looking forward to the rapidly approaching descent.

The Commando's next words served to confirm that: *Over thirteen hundred feet. It's no record in the ultrasystem, I suppose, but I bet it's in the running for a first rappel drop.* She sighed. *I'd as soon have started out with something a bit less dramatic.*

You checked the racks out?

They would go down almost in a free fall by means of rappel racks, devices consisting of a series of metal rods through which the rope was passed and compressed to control the rate of drop—speed reduced or increased as the bars were tightened or pulled farther apart. To these would be attached the seat harnesses each of them would wear to support their weight.

All too soon for Varn the meal was finished and the final examination of their gear completed.

He watched impassively as the Hadesi pulled on his harness, checked it for comfort and security, and snapped it into place. Then he was gone, and Islaen Connor was going through the same ritual.

Time seemed to suspend itself as he watched her, but at last she followed Larnse over the edge.

Islaen had also been keeping tight shields over her mind and the stomach-churning tension roiling it, but suddenly Sogan felt a rush of emotion from her, pleasure followed by a sensation akin to delight. Her feelings became even more pronounced, and it was with a considerably lighter heart that the Arcturian made his own preparations.

He clipped himself onto his rack, and taking hold of the rope, began the long descent. A moment later all his fear was back, reinforced by horror. The rope seemed to be flying through the bars of the rappel rack!

Bandit, who had gone down with Islaen, ascended to accompany him. She now whistled shrilly, radiating her alarm. *Varn, you're too fast! Go slower!*

Gripping himself, he fought down the panic starting to rise inside him. This drop, though too quick, was not perilously so, at least not at this point. He began to push the bars together. They were stiff but moved, and soon his fall slowed to an acceptable rate.

Good, the gurry told him. *You're right now.*

Varn? Islaen's thought called to him. *What happened?*

Nothing. I'd set my rack too loose, he answered and then snapped his shields into place.

Why had she done this to him? Why had she let him come to this unprepared, as if into some pleasure?

Down, ever down, he went. The sensation no longer inspired horror now that his speed was stabilized, but it remained eerie and uncomfortable for him.

Nothing about the descent was objectionable in itself. He recognized that. Progress was steady and smooth, the pace reasonable, neither painfully slow nor threateningly fast. He seemed to be floating as the walls of the great pit flowed steadily upward, and gradually both time and distance began to lose some of their hold on his perceptions.

That was part of his trouble. Sogan fought bitterly against the lessening of his grasp on the realities of his situation. He would not voluntarily surrender any of his awareness or control in this hostile place, however soft it might seem at a particular moment. He could not set aside his mistrust of it or forget those first few seconds of too-quick fall, when he had believed himself plummeting to his death far below, and his hands whitened in an ever-tightening grasp on the rappel rack.

His eyes closed. This feeling of helplessness, of utter dependence upon one slender line, was little short of agony. It was not in Varn Tarl Sogan to yield mildly to any weakness in himself. He battled against the emotions ripping the heart and manhood out of him. His will was strong and accustomed to functioning in times of danger, and knowing the greater part of his current fear to be almost entirely groundless, he was not long in bringing them under his control, even if he could not banish them entirely.

Height had never in itself been a problem for him, and he

had no trouble in looking down periodically to check his progress. Each time he did, he was gratified to find the ground perceptibly nearer. At last, after what seemed a vast age but had really been a relatively short period of time, he reached the bottom.

With considerable relief he began to unclip his harness, taking no small pleasure in the feel of solid rock beneath his feet once more. To his surprise, his hands suddenly started to shake. The tremors lasted only a moment, too briefly for him to even marshal his will to combat them or for either of the others to become aware that there was anything amiss. Still, the reaction disturbed Varn, and his mind lashed out at the Colonel, although he took care to nod in seemingly casual greeting for Greggs' benefit.

What did you mean by letting me think that was some kind of joy ride? he demanded.

But it almost was! she replied in complete astonishment. *Sure, when the fairs would come around each year on No-reen, we'd give good credits to use equipment that simulated some of the effects we experienced just now. . . .*

His expression, both of thought and feature, was so incredulous that she stopped for a moment. *Didn't young Arcturians ever have any fun?*

Plenty, but we did not classify leaping into pits as such!

Neither did we! She stopped herself. The fault was hers. She should not have been broadcasting at all, much less so foolish a sensation during a deadly serious mission.

Varn, I'm sorry to have misled you. It's probably just that I was expecting it to be so bad, and when it wasn't—

Forget it, he answered her, forcing himself to speak naturally. *I already told you I know Terrans and their seed are mad, and I have long since come to realize that Noreen's offspring are the worst of the lot.*

Bethe was almost down by then, and Jake Karmikel had begun his descent.

Sogan's already dark eyes shadowed still further as he watched the former Commando.

Karmikel's descent appeared to be well-nigh perfect. There was no amateurish burst of excessive speed from him, and probably no fear or any other distress, either. As likely as not, he was taking as much pleasure in the whole experience as Islaen had before him.

The Arcturian's face hardened. Was that not only to be expected in one of his background?

Varn turned away in disgust. The move was too abrupt, and he felt the Colonel's question even before he had completed it.

To cover himself, he sat down and leaned his back against the wall in imitation of Larnse Greggs.

"No use standing here like a pair of bloody fools," he said. "We shall probably be on our feet most of the day, and we might as well follow our guide's example and rest them while we can."

Islaen and, a few minutes later, Bethe, quickly agreed, and none of them rose again until Karmikel was almost down. All four of them got to their feet then to meet him and prepare for the next leg of their journey.

The redhead grinned broadly as he freed himself from his harness. "That was something else!"

"It wasn't bad at all," the demolitions expert agreed.

"Not bad! When I was about twelve, I would've been mad to take that trip. Of course, I'd probably have come down a whole lot faster."

"Thereby ensuring that you'd never reach thirteen," Islaen told him.

"Come on, Colonel," he said archly, "I'll bet a slew of nostalgic memories rushed into your mind as you grasped that rope. In other words, you enjoyed yourself thoroughly."

"That I did, and you well know it, you blackguard." She cast a guilty look at Sogan, but he was only laughing.

"What a pair you two make! It is a wonder either of you managed to survive even Basic training."

"Nothing was fun there," Islaen retorted, "not even the things that were supposed to be."

She felt much relieved. Varn seemed to have recovered his good humor, although he still kept tight shields on his mind. She had not at all liked the thought that she had in a way betrayed him, even in so innocent a manner. He did not need that; above all, not from her.

SIXTEEN

LARNSE GREGGS WATCHED the off-worlders as if he agreed in full with Sogan's earlier unvoiced comment regarding their sanity, but he said nothing to them.

In fact he was surprised by their reaction. He had expected that the spectacular nature of the descent would have a profounder effect on them, and perhaps even cow them, but not only had they negotiated it smoothly, they appeared to actually have taken pleasure in the experience.

The Hadesi sighed inwardly. He had imagined his far greater experience would show itself here, but that had not proven the case. Oh, his drop had undoubtedly been faster and more efficiently conducted, but no one had been below to observe that, and the difference was not significant anyway. All of the Federation party had performed well, and apart from that one too-rapid start, which had been corrected almost at once, they had worked as professionally as any Hadesi mine crew.

Larnse shrugged off his minor disappointment and took a step closer to the others, thereby fixing their attention on him.

"We're about ready to move on," he told them. "We're in an entirely different cave system now. It's wetter and has more connections with the surface. Most are very small, of no use to humans, but enough moisture washes in, including rainwater, to support enormous concentrations of wildlife."

He grimaced. "We'll be encountering examples of that, and you won't like some of them, but we'll be in no danger, not even our little feathered comrade here.

"Assuming we use even the most basic good sense and

110

enjoy reasonable fortune, we'll meet with no peril at all today and no difficulty apart from a lot of hard walking. Tomorrow we'll find the going worse, but for now we can more or less relax.''

After answering their several questions, the Hadesi took the lead, moving swiftly up the northwest corridor of the broad tunnel into which they had descended.

The walls soon began drawing together, but they never closed in to the point that the passage was unpleasant to travel, and the party stayed with it for somewhat better than an hour.

At the end of that time their guide called a halt. There was a very large break in the right-hand wall, and he pointed to it.

"This is our path. Two chambers run one into the other beyond it, both among Hades' most striking. The first is extraordinarily beautiful. The second has no prettiness but is remarkable for its size."

He led them inside.

Islaen Connor stopped, literally in midstep. "Oh!"

Whenever the beam from her lamp fell, ten thousand smaller, far-more-brilliant sparks answered it, sparks glinting with every color the human eye was capable of perceiving.

"A room of jewels," Bethe whispered in awe.

"They're only common crystals," Larnse explained, "almost valueless, and not even particularly attractive if taken from their place, but here they create a realm of pure splendor."

"No palace could equal it," Varn Tarl Sogan said softly, "not even those of legend."

All of them stood for several minutes gazing about the superb room, then regretfully began moving toward the single exit, which was situated nearly directly opposite their entrance.

They stepped through it into a sea of darkness.

"Where'd the walls go?" Jake demanded as he swept his light forward and played it right and left in a fruitless effort to find some surface to reflect it.

"They're here, Captain, but too far away for any light to reach them," Greggs told him. "I don't know what forces combined to form this chamber, but before us lies one vast emptiness. The roof soars higher than the distance we came down today, and were we to move perpendicularly to our actual course, we would require five days fast walking, without break, to traverse it from end to end. Fortunately, it's much narrower in the direction we must go, but still, we'll be a good four hours before we reach the farther side.''

His eyes went to the Colonel, as they always did when he was discussing some matter affecting their mission.

''We'll set and keep our course by compass, and we'll have to be careful to stay together. It would be very easy to get turned around once we move away from the wall, and that could mean big trouble, especially for someone alone. There are fourteen passages opening into the chamber besides those we're using for our entrance and exit, none of them leading anyplace we want to go, or, in many cases, could go.

''Also, keep on eye out as to where we're walking. The floor isn't smooth or sound in every place. There are holes, some deep enough to kill or do severe injury, but even a smaller one could be deadly. Those are especially bad since the sand covering most of the central part of the floor can hide them.''

All nodded. Down here, far from aid, even minor hurts could spell disaster, the Colonel's renewer notwithstanding. Any machine could be lost or damaged, or malfunction of its own accord.

They started out, Greggs in the lead, Varn and Islaen immediately behind him.

Jake began to follow. He took one step, another, then his knees locked. His knees and every other muscle and joint in his body. No command of will, nothing, could force him to come any farther away from the wall that was his sole contact with a sane and solid world. Beyond lay only blackness unbroken by any star. . . .

Islaen Connor snapped her shields into place so suddenly that Varn was hard-pressed not to cry out in protest at the abrupt severing of the light contact they had been maintaining between them.

He made no complaint. He had felt that rush of blind panic, or enough of it to realize she was protecting the other man as she would have protected him.

He stopped walking even before she did. Such fear could strike anyone and if it hit suddenly enough, overwhelm anyone. He had not made so fine a showing either crossing that cliff face or during the relatively safe rappel drop that he had

the right to lay fault on another for a temporary weakening
and less right still to broadcast it.

Islaen called out to Larnse. "Hold up, Mr. Greggs!"

He turned. "What's the matter?"

"Give us a minute, will you? This chamber is awesome,
and we need to get the feel of it a bit." She smiled. "You
know Hades so well that maybe the effect isn't the same for
you, but with us, each new chamber is like entering into yet
another universe, a whole new realm sometimes filled with
threat, but always with wonder."

"Of course, Colonel. I wasn't thinking, either of your
possible reaction or of our work. We should get our bearings
before venturing out into this."

The woman prayed to Noreen's gods that Karmikel would
recover quickly. Already the readings she was receiving from
him showed he was calmer, but would he be sufficiently so to
move when it became time to go on? If not, she would have
no choice but to expose what had happened to him in order to
combat it, and that she did not want to do, not before the
Hadesi.

At last Greggs proposed that they continue, and she had to
agree.

Please, Jake, her mind whispered, although she knew he
could not receive her plea.

Bethe Danlo was standing beside the redhead. She had
been nervous herself and had been staying close enough to
him to feel him freeze. Now she took his hand, twining her
fingers with his. She gently pulled him, applying steady
pressure until he followed her.

His first steps were horribly forced, as if his body were
some alien thing and no extension of his being at all, but then
the grip of his fear broke and he strode forward naturally.

Jake said nothing to the spacer, but he squeezed her hand,
acknowledging his debt to her and his gratitude. He made no
effort to release her. Rather, he shifted his hold so that their
contact might be more comfortably maintained.

For the next four hours the party walked through a realm of
utter darkness and almost total silence where even the already
soft fall of their feet was completely deadened by the blanket
of fine sand covering the cavern floor. Everywhere as far as

their lamps could penetrate, rocks and boulders were to be
seen, some of the latter of such size as to dwarf both the *Maid*
and the *Jovian Moon*.

One sound did reach them often, sometimes distinctly,
sometimes blurred, as if from a greater distance, that of
rapidly moving water. Larnse Greggs told his companions
that several small streams ran through the titanic chamber but
that they would encounter none of them on this particular
segment of their route.

There were no incidents to mar or delay their progress or
break the monotony of it. Once Greggs himself nearly stepped
into a well-hidden hole, but Islaen spotted it in time. After
that they were all more careful about where and how they set
their feet down. They spotted pits and larger holes on a
number of occasions but had no difficulty in avoiding any of
them, and counted them as no hazard at all.

In the end the sand thinned under their feet and then vanished once more. Each felt a surge of hope at its going, an
eagerness for the end of the weary march, which must now be
nearly at hand.

Time dragged more slowly then than through all the rest of
the long passage, but eventually their lights revealed the
rugged, red face of the huge cave's walls.

It was not until they were almost upon it that they spotted
the unpromising-looking slit their guide hailed as their exit.
All of them greeted it with pleasure despite its appearance and
followed him gladly through it.

Islaen Connor breathed a sigh of relief as she stepped into
the narrow corridor beyond.

An instant later that feeling was gone. Her nose wrinkled.
There was a smell. It was faint in itself, but readily perceptible and strongly contrasting with the dank odor of damp stone
to which she had long since grown accustomed. It was also
foul. Ammonia formed a large part of it, but there were other
components as well, and she wanted no part of analyzing any
of them.

All the others picked up the scent even as she had and
were turning to Greggs for an explanation.

He looked no more pleased than the off-worlders and
answered their question readily even before they could ask it.

"I warned you that we'd be running into Hades' wildlife in numbers. There's a triwing roost up ahead, a big one."

He pointed to the wall nearest them. "Where they congregate, so does just about everything else."

Islaen saw that there was quite a multitude of creatures not only on the wall, but on the floor and ceiling as well. The majority were roughly like the scavenger beetles Sogan had observed earlier, but other forms were represented—long, multilegged animals, a few fliers, and several of one species that squirmed along by undulating almost hair-thin bodies. None of them appeared to react at all either to their lights or to the heat they emitted.

Islaen was intrigued rather then repulsed and turned eagerly to Larnse. "What are they? How do they live? How do they function?"

He laughed. "One question at a time, Colonel!—They are a variety of species with long scientific names and short ones in Hadesi, none of which have been translated into Basic. Only the triwings are big enough and show themselves on the surface frequently enough to warrant that distinction.

"They live by supporting each other in life and in death. That's the way it has to be with troglobites, otherwise existence would be impossible for any of them.

"The triwings feed on whatever they find within the caverns and venture outside as well, especially during the wetter parts of the year, to graze on greenery, which they seem to require now and then in minute amounts. They much prefer native flora to our crops and take so little anyway that they've never been a problem despite their numbers.

"The rest of these creatures depend heavily although not entirely on them, eating their droppings and their bodies when they die, and their blood while they live in the case of parasites. The remainder of their support comes from material carried down with rain seepage and during the occasional floods that plague some of the cave systems.

"Except for the triwings, they never leave the caverns. They're all highly specialized populations and require the constant climate of the underworld—the damp, the cold, relatively still air, the absence of light.

"They're all blind, of course, and completely insensitive to warmth since all Hadesi creatures are cold-blooded and there's no advantage to the perception of body heat. Navigation and foraging are quite efficient processes, needless to say, and are accomplished through hearing, touch, or taste, or most commonly, through a combination of all three.''

"The triwings are different?"

"A little, since they must function for brief periods on the surface as well. They're larger for one thing, nearly as big as Bandit, and they're sighted, quite well-sighted, as a matter of fact. They get their name from a large saillike sensing organ on their backs. When it's extended, it looks exactly like a third wing.''

"Dangerous?"

He shook his head. "Not in any concentration, and believe me, Hadesim have encountered them in every conceivable number and under every conceivable condition since humans first planeted here.''

Larnse grimaced. "Just because we'll be safe and won't be with them for long doesn't mean we're going to enjoy passing through that roost. I'd advise you all to put up your hoods. All sorts of animal matter will be dropping down on us. Quite a few animals too. Triwings are constantly scratching off mites.''

Islaen hastened to free the lightweight hood from the collar pouch in her service jacket and drew it over her head. A quick glance showed that the others, including Greggs, had done the same.

She looked down at Bandit, who was riding with only her head projecting from the jacket to escape the constant chill.

"Inside, love," she instructed, pushing gently with her finger as she spoke.

She switched to mind speech after that, since no more detail could be given verbally with both Bethe Danlo and the Hadesi so near. *Get all the way under my tunic if you can. We don't want to be picking any hungry little beasties out of your feathers.*

Nooo!

I'm going to fasten my jacket. You know how to open it from the inside if you start feeling a bit cramped, don't you?

Yes. Bandit won't do it in the roost, though.

Please don't! I don't want to be picking any little beasties off me, either.

They started moving again as soon as they were all ready.

Islaen stayed close to Sogan. *Are you getting any readings?* she asked.

Plenty, most of them like those I detected around that corpse. There is a multitude of higher-level creatures ahead, but even they give me little.

Potential trouble?

No. Greggs seems to be correct there. These are not the transmissions of habitual predators. Of course, they haven't become aware of us yet.

Keep on monitoring them. Even very small animals can cause big problems if they come in large enough numbers.

He gave her a tight smile. *I am not likely to forget that, Colonel Connor. Visnu gave me far too strong a reason for remembering it.*

SEVENTEEN

THE STENCH INCREASED steadily as the party approached its source, a forty-foot circular space opening out of the corridor itself. The ceiling was a great globe at least twice that in height and many times forty feet in diameter. According to Larnse Greggs, it was fissured with a number of crevices through which its winged denizens entered and left. They appeared never to voluntarily venture into its lower reaches at all.

No individual animal was distinctly visible at that distance, but all the roof and upper walls were covered with what looked like a constantly pulsing coating, one great mass of life, ever-changing as a seemingly eternal parade of triwings took flight or settled.

The floor . . . The Commando had to fight herself to keep her stomach from twisting too violently.

It was a light brown slurry, and it, too, seethed with life. The round beetles and the long things moved on top of it and popped suddenly to the surface from someplace below. Skeletons, presumably triwing skeletons, since they were all the same and were about the right size, lay on the muck or partially buried in it, and even as she watched, a tiny, naked thing fell near her feet, an infant, she supposed, apparently already dead. Other carcasses, most half devoured or better, some still nearly whole, littered the place.

Her eyes closed. These things she could at least see. What about the rest, which had to be falling almost continuously from the vast horde above, the semiliquid feces, the urine, and those mites Greggs had mentioned?

118

There was no danger in any of it, since Hades of Persephone supported no native disease communicable to off-worlders, and there was no avoiding it either. Already, she could feel their guide steeling himself to move forward.

"How deep is that stuff?" she asked quickly as another thought came to her.

"Who knows?" he replied. "We've never measured or mined it. But to answer what I believe is your question, we won't sink into it, not more than half an inch to an inch. Two at the very most. It's quite solid underneath."

With that, he took a deep breath of the fetid air and stepped into the roosting chamber.

Islaen squared her shoulders. "Let's get it over with!"

She shuddered as the slurry squelched beneath her boots. Larnse was right. The underlayer was firm enough, but the wetter stuff on the top sloshed around her feet as she moved, throwing its contents, living and dead, over her boots.

Varn was beside her.

The thought of him drove her own revulsion from her mind. By Noreen's gentle gods, what must this be for him? She, at least, had been raised on a low-tech, agrarian world and was familiar with animals and their by-products. If she found this place so bad, she could just imagine how one bred in a palace and trained to a life aboard the Empire's proudest warships must react to it.

She glanced at him. His shields were sealed in place, of course, but his face was set in a manner she did not like, as if he were waging a battle with himself that he might well lose.

Don't let him be sick, she prayed silently. Larnse Greggs would enjoy that all too much.

Anger flared in her. No one was going to play that kind of game with her man!

Hang onto me, Varn, she told him, hoping he could hear her even if he would not—or did not dare—release his control enough to answer her. *We're almost through.*

To her surprise she did feel a linking, muffled and inarticulate, but a true mind union all the same.

Then they were out of it and all walking on solid, clean stone once more. They had been within the roost area no more than fifteen seconds.

*   *   *

Islaen quickened her pace until she had put several yards between herself and the filthy chamber, then stopped.

Varn, if there are any little beasts on us, would you please tell them to go back home?

I already have. He hesitated, then went on with a candor rare to him. *I did not like that narrow ledge we crossed yesterday, but I would sooner face it again and yet again than pass through another place like the one we just left.*

That makes a pair of us, my friend.

She felt Bandit tugging at her jacket and hastened to unfasten the second button. "Come on out, love."

The gurry flew to her shoulder, shaking herself to straighten her feathers after her confinement. *Bandit hates Hades!*

You didn't even see the roost. You'd hate it even more if you had. She reached up to caress the little creature. *Never mind that now, Bandit. Everyone's feeling down. I want you to spread a bit of cheer. Start with Jake and Bethe.*

Bandit can help?

Aye, for real. This underworld tends to get depressing for space hounds, and even at best going, we'll have to stay in it a good while longer. A visit from you would lift anyone's spirits.

It would, the hen agreed and flew off to obey.

Varn's chuckle sounded in the Commando's mind. *At least she has no doubts about her worth.*

Islaen laughed as well. *None whatsoever! The thing is, she's just about right, whereas humans sharing that trait are normally dead wrong, and insufferable besides.*

She broke off as Larnse Greggs joined them.

"I'm glad that's over," he said with feeling. "It's hard to appreciate nature's balance and variety, even on one's own world, when they take such unpleasant forms."

"Well, we got through it quickly, at any rate. I just hope we won't run into another roost."

"No, that's the only one."

His eyes flickered along the corridor before returning to her. "Have a little patience with our present state. In another half hour or so we'll be coming on a spot where the tunnel curves and widens, making a nice, broad elbow. A stream enters there, and we'll be able to wash this stuff off." He made a kicking motion with his much-soiled boot to illustrate.

"That's good to hear!"

"I thought you'd be pleased. I'd also suggest camping there. It's a bit early, but the going gets strenuous almost immediately after leaving it, and I don't think we should tackle it until we've rested."

"You know best there, Mr. Greggs. I could certainly use a break."

Islaen sighed inwardly. She wished he would give them a full account of what lay ahead instead of feeding them the details piece by piece like this, but Larnse would not reveal any information about these underground ways before they actually had to have it.

She sighed again. That caution was a throwback to the recent War, and she could not blame the Hadesim for clinging to it, not with their general mistrust of off-worlders. These tunnels had literally been life to the overrun planet, and had their secrets been broken, there could have been no effective Resistance here at all.

EIGHTEEN

As GREGGS PROMISED, the tunnel did widen, and where it did, a stream darted through a crack in the wall and hurried along the corridor in the three-foot-deep channel it had cut for itself.

All of them greeted the sight of the clear water with relief and made no delay in slipping off their packs as soon as the Commando had inspected the site and declared it satisfactory for their camp.

Islaen first washed off her boots, taking care that none of the frigid liquid should get into them, and then stripped off her jacket.

Her nose wrinkled in disgust. It, too, was soiled. Luckily, the hood and shoulder cape, which the Navy designers had just fitted to the basic garment in order to render it more serviceable, had taken the worst of it. They were totally waterproof and would rinse off easily. The remainder of the jacket also repelled moisture and stains quite efficiently, and she thought she should be able to get most of the additional mess off it without actually having to saturate it.

Their guide would fare less well. His clothing was of Hadesi design and manufacture. It was proof against damp but did not look as if it would hold back any real volume of water. He would have to keep it stretched for half the night over a plutonium disk if it was to be anything like wearable tomorrow.

She set her helmet beside her, to better position the light for exposing the various marks, and loosened the neck fastenings of her tunic. The water was punishingly cold, but she was not going to let that drive her off. It was too good a chance to wash away some of the sweat and grime of their journey, and she wouldn't let it be wasted because of momentary discomfort.

The others were all engaged in more or less the same business, all except Bandit, who had removed herself as far as she could from the icy stream and was preening herself after the fashion of her kind.

Sogan, too, had moved away from his companions. Islaen had expected he would. It was only a matter of a few feet, but the best he could do without making his withdrawal too obvious. He would want to wash and dress again quickly, counting on the shadows and their own preoccupation to keep the others from becoming aware of his back.

Her eyes lowered. It was nothing like it had been before the Navy physicians on Horus had turned their renewers on it, but it was still bad, more than sufficient to give an unsuspecting observer a nasty shock. The sight of it certainly would cause him to be remembered, which the Arcturian still wished to avoid, although he knew now that his own people would not come hunting him if he were identified. Then, too, he was self-conscious about his scars, and preferred to keep them hidden for that reason as well.

Poor Varn, she thought sympathetically. He had found little of pleasure on this excursion. Let him at least be spared that embarrassment. Since he had been so insistent about coming with them, he had literally asked for anything that had happened to him down here, but she did not have it in her to be insensitive to his discomfort.

Larnse Greggs watched the Commando sullenly. He felt annoyed with the entire party. They were adapting too well and functioning too well. It did not seem right that a pack of off-worlders should be having as easy a time in Hades' underworld as one of her own sons.

That was irrational, he knew. They had all done their share of struggling and had all experienced their share of trouble. He scowled at the Commando. She was no more to blame than any of the others, but she was their leader and thus the focus of his ill feeling toward them.

His lips tightened into a bitter line as he glanced at Sogan. She had also teamed with that dark-eyed image of an Arcturian, he thought. The son of a Scythian ape seemed to believe himself too good to remain with his own comrades when he had a chance to be away from them—him with his talk of palaces. What would a space hound or a mere Navy Captain know about those, anyway?

He looked at Islaen in disgust. How could a woman like this, one who had proven her worth many times over, have so degraded herself as to link herself with something like that?

As Greggs watched, she bent farther over the stream. Something slipped out from beneath her tunic, a pendant of some sort suspended from what looked to be a gold or fauxgold chain.

It was a jewel, he saw, a large one and extraordinarily beautiful.

The Hadesi's eyes widened as he recognized it for what it was. A river tear! He might never have seen one before, but few people in all the ultrasystem, and certainly no one from a planet with a significant mining industry, would fail to know what they looked like.

There was but a couple of feet separating them, and he was upon her in the next instant, slamming a vicious blow straight into her face before she could so much as react to the sudden surge of his fury, much less raise any defense.

"Whore!" he snarled furiously. "You let the bastard buy you!"

He aimed a second blow at the stunned woman, but before he could deliver it, before even Jake could come to her aid, Varn Tarl Sogan struck.

He used no blaster. Officers of the Arcturian Empire were trained to require no mechanical weapons either to defend themselves or to slay, and he had learned still other techniques during his months of association with the Commandos. Strong, unconventional fighter though Larnse Greggs was, he could not withstand the inconceivable fury of this assault, particularly after having been taken unawares by it. He knew a few moments of agony and terror, then unconsciousness mercifully claimed him and he had no further knowledge of the punishment his battered body was taking.

"You'll kill him, you bloody fool!"

Karmikel knew the former Admiral did not hear him. Quickly stepping behind him, he joined his hands into a double fist and struck Sogan once and then again hard on the back of the head. The second blow brought the Arcturian to the ground.

Jake looked around for Bethe as he knelt beside Greggs, and saw she had already gone to the Colonel. "How is she?"

"Just stunned. She's coming around."

"Good. Get her renewer. This son's in a bad way."

"What about Sogan?" she asked as she ran to obey.

"He should be all right, worse luck to him. I don't think I hit him all that hard."

The spacer quickly located the renewer and brought it to Karmikel. She studied Larnse with concern. "He looks done, Jake."

"Well, the right arm's smashed, and I doubt he has a sound rib left. The renewer can take care of all that, but if the lungs are shredded, it'll only do a temporary patch at best. That'd be a job for a regrowth."

He scowled at the felled Arcturian. "We were just lucky he didn't go for the abdominal cavity first, or Greggs'd be as good as dead, if not dead already.—See if I broke his neck, like I should've done, will you?"

Islaen sat up then. She wiped some of the blood from her face as she stared at the scene before her in sheer horror. Bethe came over and helped her to her feet, giving her a terse account of what had occurred.

The Commando ignored Sogan. She hastened to where Jake was working on Greggs. "Well?"

He glanced up. "I don't know. The renewer'll fix up the broken bones, but I wish I knew if any of the organs are smashed or punctured."

His eyes met hers as he spoke. Islaen Connor could not only read human emotion, she could examine a human body, discover any injury and most ailments, even those of which the victim himself was unaware. He was asking her to use that aspect of her power now.

Islaen knelt to check Greggs' vital signs. As she did her mind went out from her, and after a few seconds she gave the former Commando a smile and a barely perceptible nod. The Hadesi had suffered no damage beyond their ability to repair.

"All the signs check," she said aloud. "I think we've lucked out. Just keep at it with the renewer."

She went to her consort and performed a similar examination on him.

He too was all right. Although still unconscious, he had taken no injury apart from a swelling already rising at the base of his head. She freed her canteen from her belt and emptied its contents onto his face.

Varn groaned and sat up, holding his head in his hands. He looked at her. *Islaen—Your face! Greggs—*

That last was a hiss, but she cut it off. "Just shut up, will you? He's alive, no thanks to you."

She refused to open her mind to his. All her anger both at the attack on her and the chaos that had followed flared up. "Of all the moronic stunts I've ever seen played, this has to be given the grand prize! Do you realize how close you came to putting an end to this mission and maybe 300,000 innocent lives along with it? You knew he was unstable and that we had to hold control of the situation."

"I had provocation. . . ."

"Provocation? You've had provocation before! All your life you've conducted yourself as if you're barely one step up from a machine, and you have to pick now to break loose?"

She shook her head as she made an effort to contain her fury, then gave way to it again. "You're not hurt. Just get out of my sight and stay out of it!"

Islaen started back to Greggs but thought better of it when she saw he was coming around as well. Instead she went to sit by the bank of the stream. The sight of her might set him off again and maybe cause renewed damage to his recently repaired injuries. She did not bother to check or care to know what Sogan did or where he went.

Larnse Greggs' eyes focused on the two anxious and very angry faces looking down at him. He shuddered violently, remembering vividly that living image of death he had last seen.

"I was sure he'd kill me."

"You were lucky. He wanted to break every bone in your body before he did, and he was well on the way to succeeding." Jake shook his head. "I've known Sogan a lot of years, but I have never seen him lose control of himself before."

His blue eyes flashed in sudden fury and transfixed the

other man. "If he hadn't, I might well have. Islaen's his wife, but she's my friend."

"All right, Jake," Bethe told him quietly. "That's not going to help any of us. Take the renewer over to Islaen. She won't want to be walking around with her face in that state."

Once they were alone, the demolitions expert turned to Larnse. "Why, Greggs?"

He took a moment to answer but did so in the end. His anger had nearly destroyed their mission, betrayed Karst. The woman had at least a right to an explanation. "That jewel," he said. "She had to have gotten it from him."

"That's none of your concern! It's also an extremely broad assumption."

He gave a cold laugh. "She didn't buy it on a Commando's salary."

"Maybe, maybe not, but she has a brace of class-one heroism citations and shares another with Sogan, remember? That's a lot of credits. She doesn't have to put anything into their ship with the Navy keeping her in trim for them, and she—both of them—would be looking around for a suitable investment. A jewel like that would be ideal. Most spacers put whatever extra funds they can amass into the best stones they can find."

She scowled at him. "They work the rim too. Every assignment Islaen's team has had since the War has been out here. Who knows how fortune may have risen for them? I thought even a planet hugger like you knew that can happen and does happen frequently enough to draw spacers and hold us, despite all the hard work and the danger and the some-times awesome loneliness."

His head lowered. "I never considered that."

"Obviously."

"It seems I owe her . . ."

"That puts it somewhat mildly, but let it rest for the moment. We all need time to cool down before starting any discussion, Islaen Connor included."

Islaen gratefully accepted Jake's ministrations with the ray and then washed the drying blood from her face.

"How do I look?" she asked him when she had finished.

He smiled. "Beautiful. There's no sign that anything happened to you. Except for your clothes, of course. There's more blood on them than there was on your face.''

''They'll be cleaned after this jaunt, if they're worth salvaging.''

She pressed her fingers to her eyes. ''I can't believe all this happened, Jake.''

His hand closed over hers. ''It's over now,'' he said gently. ''Just take it easy for a while. Bethe's playing peacemaker right now with Greggs.''

''Varn?''

''He's retreated up the tunnel. You can just see him from here,'' Karmikel told her when she did not turn her head, ''He loves you, Islaen. I didn't realize how much until now. He would've taken any insult or any injury to himself.''

The war prince had struck with a similar fury when those young thugs had slightly injured her in an attempt to waylay them on Set of Isis, she recalled. He had retained more control over himself then, but that attack had been impersonal in itself and there had been no history of hostility behind it.

No matter! An officer knew better than to let his temper rule him. Varn Tarl Sogan had both failed and disappointed her.

''We would've been better served by a somewhat less intense devotion,'' she replied sourly.

She suddenly forgot the Arcturian entirely. ''Oh, Bandit!''

The gurry fluttered to the ground beside her. She was trembling so violently that she had scarcely been able to make the short flight.

Islaen scooped her up, cradling her protectively in her cupped hands. ''My poor little love! This was a thousand times worse for you than for any of the rest of us, but it's ended now. No one's been permanently hurt. Even Greggs is mended.''

Varn's very unhappy, she managed to say after several attempts.

That reminder aroused Islaen's anger once more. ''Varn should be unhappy.''

The gurry's answering moan softened her again.

''You're right, though, little Bandit. This can't go on, or we'll never accomplish anything.''

Sighing, she got to her feet. The hen made a valiant effort

to rally herself and take her normal perch on the Commando's shoulder, but Islaen's fingers closed gently around her, confining her.

"No, love. Varn and I must speak alone this time. You stay with Jake. He'll take care of you until we come back."

"That I will, and with pleasure." He paused. "Good luck, Colonel."

"Thanks, friend. I may need it.—Maybe if he's miserable enough, I'll actually get a few answers out of him," she added, speaking more to herself than to him.

Islaen found the Arcturian leaning against the tunnel wall, his back to the camp, staring into the darkness ever looming just beyond the beam of his lamp.

Varn?

Aye, Colonel?

He did not turn, and she steeled herself. There was no defiance on him, just an almost infinite shame.

Please, Varn. I shouldn't have reamed you like I did, but I—I can't always be strong for you.

Sogan faced her then. *You have had to be many times, I think. Maybe too many.—I know what I did just now and what the cost might have been.*

His eyes closed. *I have been wrong since the beginning of this, wrong in insisting on coming with you, criminally wrong in doing so after that first encounter with Greggs showed us what he was.*

He seemed vulnerable, as if he had no defenses left. Perhaps he was so dispirited, she thought, that he had in fact set them aside. She reached out to him but dropped her hands when she saw him stiffen against her, as if he feared the contact would sully her.

The past is over, she told him, *and what was to come of it has, but why? What made you demand a place on a mission like this, especially at first, when it all seemed so simple a task?*

He would not look at her.

Karmikel.

Jake? Islaen asked in bewilderment.

I knew he would never let you go down alone, and I did not want you two working together as you had in the past, not unless I could be there as well.

She straightened. *We were never more than comrades!*

Nor would you ever be. I know your vow is binding, Islaen Connor. It was not that which I feared.

What, then?

I know how poorly I match with either of you in any surplanetary work, and we have been married long enough now for any mystique which might have surrounded me in your eyes to have dissipated. I did not want to give you a chance to return again to your old customs and—

He stopped, but forced himself to go on in the next instant. *And to realize the mistake you had made.*

She stared at him incredulously, then fought down paralyzing amazement. She had to answer him, and immediately. *How I wish I had known this,* she told him softly. *Varn, what grief I could have spared you!*

I could not speak of it. Even now, when my temper has made it necessary that you be told. . . .

This time, she placed her hand on his arm despite his unspoken protest. *It's a man that I love, not—not an incarnation of some god. It was a man I loved on Thorne.*

She looked back at the camp. *We should rejoin the others. We have to continue with this.*

It might be best if I remain behind or went back altogether.

She shook her head emphatically. *No. That would just give Greggs a victory of sorts, that of driving you off. I need him, but I'm not about to grant him any favors.*

I failed you once, he reminded her.

Not precisely. I laid more blame on you than you should rightly have to bear. If you hadn't acted fast, he could well have killed me before Jake came to my rescue, or smashed me up beyond the renewer's ability to repair.—Varn, I need you. You will fail me in truth if you won't back me now.

I am with you, whenever and in whatever manner you will, Islaen Connor.

NINETEEN

THEY FOUND LARNSE GREGGS sitting up, braced against the wall for support, when they reached the others.

I'll have to talk to him, the Commando said without any enthusiasm, *but I think you should keep aloof for a while. I don't want him set off again.*

Sogan frowned. *What if he does explode? Your gift did not warn you before.*

I wasn't monitoring him. I got careless. However, you'll be standing in easy range, with your blaster set to stun.

She eyed him speculatively. *Don't use it if you can help it. I don't want to stress his system any more, after the shocks it's already received.*

I will take care. His eyes were so dark as to seem nearly black. *Suppose he attacks you again, Islaen?*

Then we obviously cannot continue with the mission according to our present plan. I'll have to send Bethe and Jake on with him while you and I go back to the surface.

Her eyes sparked. *If that happens, by all the gods, I'll see him pay the price. I'll see the leaders of this place as soon as we reach Karst. Hadesim are not forgiving of weakness, particularly of this magnitude and when duty is violated as a result of it. He'd be a ruined man and maybe an exile to boot.*

She gripped herself. *That probably won't come to pass. Right now he's feeling nearly as badly as you are, though he has full cause for it.*

Bracing herself so that she should remain impassive before her assailant, the Commando strode over to where Greggs was sitting. "You are well now?" she asked without any pretense of warmth.

131

"Aye, Colonel."

She could feel him steel himself, gather his courage to continue speaking. "Colonel Connor, in my imagination I lay a number of deeds a Hadesi holds to be most vile against you, and then I responded to those imaginings with physical deed. For that I can only beg your forgiveness. For the danger I thereby put on our mission and on Karst, there can be no such grace. I expect to feel the weight of my stupidity when we return to the surface."

His mouth twisted. "If the Resistance had conducted itself as I have these last days, Hades would soon have been left without an army and probably without a populace as well."

"What occurs on a Commando mission generally remains part of that mission alone," she replied. "There will be no report against you, provided we have no further trouble.

"Rest now. I want an early start tomorrow, as if there were an early or late in this hole," she added bitterly. "The sooner we finish our work, the sooner we can all be away from here."

Their normal rising hour found the party already ready to go.

Islaen approached Greggs. "According to what you originally told us, this should be our last full day. Is there any chance we might reach the arsenal today if we pushed?"

He shook his head. "Not much. We won't be able to make any speed at all. The stream will continue with us almost the whole way. The tunnel narrows beyond this point, and we'll have to travel straddling the channel. Barring foul luck, a slip'll mean no more than a wet foot, but it's hard work, and it's slow."

He paused. "At the end of that come two tight spots. Really tight. The more I think about them, the more worried I become. I'll get through, and you women will, but the men are considerably bigger, especially Karmikel. I'm simply not sure they can make it."

"We'll just have to make it, won't we?" Jake growled.

"No," Varn Tarl Sogan said quietly. "If there is a possibility that we cannot negotiate one of those passages, we had best face it now. To become irredeemably trapped could seal the return against the others as well as doom ourselves."

"What do you suggest?" Bethe asked, watching him both curiously and with considerable respect.

"That we proceed with the intention of reaching the arsenal, naturally. If that proves impossible, we will wait a certain amount of time for your return and then go back the way we came, with or without you, and bring report of that other party's presence down here. We have ascenders and know the theory of their use. Jake has actually trained with them as well, I believe."

The former Commando nodded. "We'll be able to manage them."

Greggs gave them a sharp look. "You could find your way to the rope? With no guide?"

"Commandos can function on their own. We wouldn't last long if we couldn't," Karmikel answered carefully, not wishing to reveal they had been mapping Hades' secret routes, an effort they had managed to conceal thus far, lest more trouble rise out of it, "and the way's pretty straightforward, not too many twists or turns. We shouldn't have a problem with it."

Islaen Connor looked from him to Varn. "Very well, but let's just hope it doesn't come to that. Even at full strength I fear the pirates will have a numerical advantage over us if we run into them."

Her eyes caught Larnse's. "That's the chief reason I was hoping we could get in there early—to beat them to the planetbuster and be away again before they got to the arsenal at all."

"We can't be that sure about their timing, Colonel," he pointed out, "not when we don't even know precisely when they came into the caves, and I'm warning you, we cannot completely tire ourselves out before reaching that crawl. We'll never make it through if we do. It's going to take everything we've got as it is."

"So be it, then," she said with a resigned sigh. "You know Hades' ways."

She lifted her pack and squirmed it into place on her shoulders. "Let's be off, comrades."

The following hours were as tiring and tedious as Larnse Greggs had predicted they would be. Chiefly they traveled with one foot on each narrow ledge that passed for the banks of

the small stream. Twice, when the stream bed widened to a point
where they could no longer straddle it, they were forced to
creep along one side, clutching the wall for support. Once, they
rested, sitting with their legs stretched across the cleft in
the tunnel floor and their feet braced on the opposite bank,
the little river running merrily beneath them.

There were no incidents, not even a slip, but none of them
grew weary of the monotony or of the hard work entailed in
this method of travel. Their minds were too firmly fixed on
what lay ahead.

The end of that phase of their labors came abruptly when
the sundered floor suddenly united once more.

Bethe Danlo stared at the solid, smooth expanse of damp-
darkened red stone incredulously and with some suspicion.
"What happened to the stream?" she asked of no one in
particular.

Larnse smiled faintly. "It's under our feet, flowing through
a sump, a flooded tunnel below us. It'll rejoin us later, but
we're lucky it vanishes here. Otherwise we'd have no back
door into the arsenal."

The Hadesi pointed to a horizontal slit in the left-hand
wall. It was about a foot above the floor, a foot wide, and
scarcely half that in height. They could not imagine even a
child getting through that space.

Their thoughts were not difficult for Greggs to read. He
shook his head. "It's not as small as it seems from this angle.
We're looking at an overhang. The actual entrance is made
from underneath."

He knew this would not hold any of them back from
making the attempt and went on. "For the most part we're
facing a straight, tight crawl, but right at the beginning, only
ten feet in, there's a bad jog, a sharp bend coming at a hump
in the floor. In order to get past it, we'll have to turn onto our
backs to work our knees and hips around and over it. After
that we'll be finished with the acrobatics. There are no more
major blocks, but we'll have to watch for the places where
the roof dips down. Anyone who gets careless and strikes one
of those could well find himself stuck, or brain himself. We'll
be pushing our helmets before us as well as our packs. There
isn't the headroom to allow for them in there."

This announcement provoked a chilled silence, which Islaen Connor broke after a moment. "How long is the crawlway?"

"Two hundred twelve feet," he informed her, "and it's a bad drag the whole way. If there's been any kind of a fall at all, it'll be a demon's own pit for a fact."

"Fall?" she asked sharply.

"The crawl formed in the bed of an old river. There's a lot of small stuff in the walls and roof—pebbles, hunks of rock, even soil of a sort. It comes down now and then, not a lot, but it doesn't take much to render that wormhole impassible."

"If we find that has happened?" Jake demanded.

"We'll have to clean it out. It's not impossible. Hadesi units had to do it several times during the War and still managed to arm themselves in time to carry out planned raids."

"I'd prefer to avoid imitating them," Islaen remarked grimly. "We've enough ahead of us without that."

Greggs gave her a measuring look. "We should change our order of march, putting both your men last. We'll have accomplished nothing if Danlo winds up sealed on the wrong side of the crawl."

Varn Tarl Sogan felt Islaen's distaste for that suggestion and her acknowledgment of the cold reality supporting it.

"He is right," he agreed quickly. "Refusing to accept the dangers we face will not lessen them, and refusal to do what we might to minimize their effects could bring disaster to our purpose as well as to individual victims."

"So be it," Islaen replied, her head lowered. "Any more suggestions, Greggs?"

The guide nodded. "We three can follow one another pretty closely, but it would be advisable for Karmikel and Sogan to come one at a time after we've won free. It's not an entirely necessary precaution, but it could help prevent a second disaster if one of them should get stuck."

To this, too, the Commando agreed.

Larnse slipped his pack from his shoulders. "Look," he said, addressing the two off-world men directly for the first time, "all this is preparation for possible problems, not an anticipation of them. Just take your time, rest frequently, and keep your wits about you, and we should all come through fine."

TWENTY

VARN PUSHED HIS way in and up, bending his body to bring it onto the main crawlway. He lay there for a couple of seconds to accustom himself to his surroundings.

The light was almost uncomfortably bright, although he had dimmed his lamp to the minimum extent possible. With the pack filling most of the passage in front of him, better than ninety percent of the beam was reflecting either off it or the stone immediately around him.

He shuddered. There had been other lights in that first crawlspace they had traversed, but he had no companion in here. He was alone, utterly, absolutely alone, in the long, narrow hole that might become his tomb if fortune willed against him.

The war prince started forward, inching his way along as best he might. Within minutes he began to feel the strain of such movement and recognized the wisdom, the stark necessity, of complying with Greggs' suggestion that they rest often. Even with that, he knew he would be battling for every millimeter's advance by the end of the crawl.

At least the most difficult challenge would come soon, he thought with relief. Better to have it over at once and not be forced to endure the pangs of anticipation on top of the concrete discomforts the passage presented.

The tunnel altered course so suddenly that he might have struck the corner wall had he been giving less than his full attention to the way before him. Carefully, he maneuvered his pack around the sharp bend and manipulated his helmet to gain the best view possible of what lay ahead.

His lips tightened. It looked bad.

The three who had entered before had made it. He began wriggling ahead again, twisting onto his side at the turn, then onto his back as he crossed over the hump, allowing his knees to bend with the sharp angle of the passage.

Once, his pack lodged, and he knew an instant of dread, but he freed it again in a couple of seconds. It was smaller, much smaller, than he was, and he knew he should have no trouble with it apart from the inconvenience of propelling it along before him. He had worse than that to concern him.

It did not take him long to make his way through the twisted place, despite the maneuvering required, and soon the Arcturian lay on his stomach once more with a clear, straight passage stretching out before him.

He raised himself the little he could to peer over his pack at the way ahead. His dark eyes were bleak. A wormhole, Larnse Greggs had called it. An apt name, he thought; perhaps too apt. Certainly it was no passage created for human use. He was an alien thing here, an invader too large and too clumsy to function within it, and so ultimately doomed.

His eyes closed, then opened again. He had more to do than give his fancy rein like this, he told himself angrily.

Sogan brought his wrist to his lips and activated the tiny instrument fastened to it. Commandos had used the incredibly tough personnel communicators throughout the War, and found them equally useful on their current missions. Although not technically classified, the basically secretive guerrillas preferred not to make any unnecessary display of them, and neither he nor Islaen would have thought to use theirs between themselves on this assignment, even had they lacked a far better means of communication.

Conditions were different now. Jake Karmikel had been permitted to keep his along with most of his gear upon demobilization, since he had declared his willingness to serve with the military in case of need. They were essentially alone, and the former Admiral had proposed he report on potential problem areas as he encountered them, so that the Noreenan would have at least a working knowledge of the tunnel before he had to enter it. Jake was a little surprised Sogan had been issued one of the communicators despite his connection with Islaen, but he had been quick to agree to the idea.

This was Varn's first transmission. He described the section he had just passed through and gave his estimate that the other man should have little more trouble with it than he had, and maybe less in view of his more appropriate training.

That done, he turned his attention back to the passage itself.

His progress was slow. He had known it must be, yet he detested this place so much that he drove himself to get through, stopping less frequently and for shorter stretches than was wise, certainly not nearly often enough to counter the weariness building in him.

He had to break free! All he had felt in that first crawlway returned to him again, but where that had triggered the easily ignored working of superficial imagination, this was a venom poisoning all his being.

There was no way to escape it. How could he, with the cold, life-hating stone scraping at his shoulders, his hair, as he dragged himself along? At times he came close to believing the tunnel was a malignant spirit, waiting to clasp him in an unyielding embrace of death—a slow death of want or cold in the eternal dark, far from the stars and the disciplined yet wild freedom of space.

Varn stopped suddenly. Did the tunnel look different?

His spirits leaped high. The passage snaked into a very gentle S-curve just ahead of him. This was what he had been waiting to see. The exit was now not ten yards distant.

He nearly threw himself forward, anticipation giving a strength to his weary muscles that he would not have believed they still possessed. Soon, now, he would be out of it, out and with Islaen—

His shoulders struck rock. Wincing, he pushed on in annoyance. He gained a few more inches but then stopped. Stopped dead. He could neither go on nor, he discovered a moment later to his horror, could he retreat.

The stone gripped him like a vise. Its hold was punishing, biting his shoulders, compressing his chest and back. He knew what had happened. Too late he recalled the warning that the passage narrowed drastically here. Instead of carefully working his way through, he had rammed himself right into it; now, like a cork stoppering a flask of wine, he was held. Here he would be held.

Panic ripped through him, but now his old pride and will to fight rose up as well. If he was to die, even in this wretched place, in this manner, he would die as befit a war prince of the Arcturian Empire. In the meantime, he was not prepared to tamely surrender himself.

Varn Tarl Sogan considered his position carefully. He seemed to be trapped, but he had gotten into this place. The walls had not fallen or shrunk around him, and so it should be possible to extricate himself again, although perhaps at the cost of considerable bruising.

That last warranted no consideration at all. The Arcturian compelled his body to relax. Very cautiously he tried a few exploratory movements.

He nearly cried out aloud in his relief. He was not free, not by a far sight, but neither was he held fast. He could move, however little.

Sogan exhaled, forcing every particle of air that he could from his lungs until he began to grow dizzy from the effort.

Suddenly he felt the jaws of the rock release. He had broken Hades' deadly trap!

In another few minutes he was entirely free, but was it to go forward or back? He was torn for one terrible instant of indecision, then he began to advance. To return was to experience once more all the fear, the misery, the monstrous effort. It would have to be endured again at the completion of their task, of course, but if he gave in now, without so much as attempting to try to reach the arsenal, the shame of his defeat would flay him as sharply as the lashes of his people once had. He knew now that retreat was possible should this final tight stretch prove impassible, but challenge it he must.

He worked his way onward millimeter by millimeter until at last the tunnel widened around him. It was by a couple of precious inches only, but that was enough. He had sufficient space to maneuver if he exercised only reasonable caution, and he had won. He would have no further trouble in the short distance left for him to crawl.

Varn lay his sweat-damp face on his arm, for a moment too weak with relief and exhaustion of both body and spirit to move, but he was not long in resuming command over himself. He had broadcast his terror when he had first discovered he was trapped, and had been broadcasting all his efforts to free himself. Islaen had not attempted to contact him then, fearing to distract him, but she knew the danger was now over. She had the courtesy to grant him time to collect himself, but he could feel her questions, her concern, the aftertaste of her fear for him. It was his to reassure her.

Islaen, he called gently, inviting and welcoming her touch. *It is over now. There is no more cause for worry.*

Varn! Praise the Spirit of Space! What happened?

I got stuck, entirely through my own carelessness, but I have managed to work myself free again. As soon as I warn Jake not to repeat my mistakes, I shall be hurrying on to join you.

Not too fast! she cautioned. *It's still tight in there.*

I think I have learned that lesson well, Colonel Connor, he replied dryly.

Shall I stay with you?

Sogan hesitated. He wanted that, the warmth and light of her mind's presence, but he decided against her offer.

You had best withdraw, Colonel. After this adventure, I think I shall do better by keeping all my wits fixed on what I am doing. That would be a difficult task with you too near me.

Have it your way, Admiral.

She spoke lightly, matching the tone of her response to his. It was difficult to imagine how Varn Tarl Sogan could rally like this so quickly after what she had felt him experience, but he had. Now it was her part to support his strength as he had chosen to display it.

TWENTY-ONE

JAKE KARMIKEL STUDIED the way ahead of him. His progress had been slow and difficult, but he had suffered no mishaps thus far, in great part thanks to the information he had received from the former Admiral. Sogan had seen to it that there had been no surprises to unbalance or trap him.

Now, however, for the first time since entering this miserable tunnel, he was uncertain, not of what he faced, but whether he should attempt it at all.

His expression was hard, tense. Just before him lay the deceptively gentle-looking S-curve where Varn Tarl Sogan had nearly come to grief. How close it had been, he did not know, but he had no doubt whatsoever that the trouble had been potentially very serious. The Arcturian had described the incident just a shade too lightly for it to be otherwise.

Jake could see the place where Sogan had been held. The ancient sediment comprising the wall was roughened there, and a few pebbles had even been pulled loose.

The sight chilled him. If the smaller man had so very nearly been caught, what hope at all had he?

Still, a great part of it had been the other's fault, as he had freely confessed. He had attempted to use thoughtless force and speed where he should have finessed his way through, as his later success had proven, and he had reported that care should bring Karmikel through as well.

The Noreenan studied the tight place for several minutes longer with growing unease, but at last decided to give it a try. Like Varn before him, he could not face the return—in a backward crawl, at that—if he could possibly gain the exit.

He cautiously approached the curve, started to enter it. His heart gave a painful jolt as he felt the walls grip him, but he forced himself to remain calm. He had stopped at the first hint of undue pressure, and so had not jammed himself. He followed Sogan's example and began a series of small, gentle movements while exhaling to reduce the size of his chest.

It worked even more quickly than it had for his more gravely trapped predecessor, and he was soon moving forward again.

Relief replaced concern when his upper body at last cleared the treacherous spot, although he relaxed none of his caution. That had been the final challenge. He should be out now within a relatively few minutes.

Disaster struck without any warning. He was just drawing his legs past Hades' would-be death trap when a rock, imperfectly embedded in the disturbed wall and loosened by the exertions of the two men, suddenly tore free and struck squarely on the Noreenan's leg.

It was a sliver of stone, very slender, but long and surprisingly heavy. One end wedged against his calf just above the ankle, the other firmly against the wall from which it had broken.

Only the powerful control instilled in him during the long years of almost constant peril kept Jake from crying out in pain and surprise. As the initial white-hot surge of agony subsided a little, he realized his leg was probably not broken. The pain, though intense enough, was not of that nature. The major blood vessels, particularly the artery, were probably sound as well, he decided, or he would be feeling the effect of lost blood even now.

As for the rest, he could but guess. The space was so small, and he was so positioned and confined, that he could not see the thing that held him.

Once more the former Commando resorted to fine movement, fighting to ignore the vastly intensified pain, but it was to no avail. He could not budge the stone. A savage kick with his free leg only jammed it more tightly into his tormented flesh, driving him to the brink of unconsciousness.

His mind struggled against oblivion, ease though it would have been, and gradually the enveloping mists cleared away. Karmikel's eyes closed, but he retained his grip on himself.

He was trapped. That he must acknowledge, and he must accept all it portended. They had all known this could happen. Now it was up to him to follow through with the duty fate had set on him.

At least he still had use of his arms, he thought wearily, as he brought his communicator to his lips. They were of no help to him now, but he doubted his sanity could have borne it if he had been deprived of them as well, if they had somehow been pinned, straitjacket fashion, to his sides.

He had no other means of informing his comrades of what had befallen him, and so activated the little communications instrument on the general frequency. Islaen Connor's reply came in the next moment, calmly, although he knew she must be reading his fear and pain. She would have been aware that he was in trouble from the moment the accident had occurred.

Schooling himself to speak dispassionately, he described his position. Only at the end did his voice threaten to betray him, but he managed to hold it steady.

"I'm afraid you'll have to take that planetbuster out all by yourselves. I'm going to have to content myself with waiting here and getting the details when you come back and pull me out."

After that he carefully closed the transmission switch and buried his face in his arm.

All four, off-worlders and Hadesi alike, stared in stunned horror at the communicator on the Colonel's wrist.

"We can't get back to him, not in time," Greggs judged, voicing the thought of all. "Hypothermia works faster than that. He'll be dead long before we can work our way around to reach him."

"Jake knows that," Islaen said quietly.

The guide's face was grim. The dangers and terrors of Hades' underworld were part of him, and so, too, was the aid the members of a team rendered to one another when peril threatened any of their number in these caves. It violated his every instinct to walk away from a man in such a situation and abandon him to certain, slow death, but he saw no way to save Jake Karmikel.

"If that rock had come down on one of his arms, we might have been able to do something," he muttered in a voice made fierce by frustration, "but we can do nothing with the whole length of his body between us and it."

"Maybe, maybe not," the Commando snapped. "We don't really know how badly he's trapped, do we? Jake couldn't tell us, and if he's hurting as badly as I think he is, the pain would be overriding his tactile senses. I'll go back there, haul out his pack, and then have a good look at how things actually stand."

"No, I'll do it," Bethe Danlo interrupted quickly. "I'm the smaller of us. I'll be able to make it faster."

Islaen nodded. "Go ahead."

The spacer wasted no further time. She dropped to her knees beside the exit hole and squirmed inside. "Jake!" she called. "Jake, I'm coming in. Cut your lamp when you spot my light and watch your own eyes. No point in letting the glare dazzle you."

She gave her attention to her work then. It was no easier than on her first time through, and no more pleasant, but she knew she would not have to endure it for very long.

Bethe reached the trapped man in a pathetically short time. He had come so far before fortune had struck him down. . . .

She masked both her sorrow and her fear. "I'm going to take your pack out first and come back for a real look at you. The way it is now, all I can see is a rather begrimed mop of red hair."

"Don't waste your time, Bethe, or the others'," the former Commando told her gently, although he desperately did not want her to leave him. "Bravado aside, we all know I'm done."

"None of that, Jake Karmikel!" she flared. "Not yet, at any rate. Islaen wouldn't have gotten to be a Colonel in the Commandos if she weren't a pretty resourceful character, and you can bet Greggs knows how to manage an emergency as well, after having spent nearly all his life in the Resistance, so don't go giving up on us yet."

"Very well, Sergeant," he replied meekly, according her her former rank.

"I'll be back in a few minutes." She hesitated. "Shall I bring you something for the pain?"

"No," he answered. "If there is a chance, you may need my cooperation. I'd best keep my wits about me."

Hope was beginning to stir within him despite all logic. Islaen Connor had won their team out of so many situations where death should have been the only possible end . . .

As she had promised, the demolitions expert quickly returned to Jake. She took his hands in hers and kissed them softly, then lifted her eyes to meet his.

The smile she gave him was bright, although her heart was heavy. He felt so cold already, and she feared that even at best, his ordeal would not end for a long time to come.

She raised herself to the fullest extent possible to study the spire of stone pinning him to the ground.

Bethe wanted to cry openly in her despair, but the sight of the Noreenan's pain-ravaged face sealed her resolve to hold firm. The hope she had so cruelly revived in him was false. She knew that now, after having seen how the rock was fixed, but she would let him keep the comfort of it a brief while longer, until she returned with the pain suppressant. Jake would then realize the truth himself, but the dose she would give him would be a strong one. He would soon sleep, and would remain asleep until he passed from this state into that other one.

Her grasp tightened for a moment before she very gently slipped her hands away from his. "I have to report to the others now, but I won't leave you alone for too long."

Jake nodded. He had hoped for more, but that was unrealistic. He knew his situation was bad, that he should not have anticipated an instantaneous solution. He would just have to wait for the others' response. Bethe Danlo was right. Theirs was a resourceful company, and they would be able to think of a way to release him, if anyone could. He sighed then and shuddered violently, only partly from the cold gripping him. If anyone could . . .

The spacer's hand raised in farewell as she began backing down the ill-starred tunnel yet another time. She tried to keep from her mind the thought that when she next left him, Jake Karmikel would already be in the sedation-induced sleep that was the first step of his descent into death.

She lowered her eyes as he activated his lamp once more, and was glad that she had. Tears were welling up in them despite her efforts to will them away, and she did not want him to become aware of them. Increasing distance helped, and her lamp—too bright even at this low setting in so confined a space—would serve to blind him to fine detail even as the tears blurred her vision.

So much light, it seemed, and yet it was nothing, less than a spark, when set against the infinity of darkness around them.

A spasm of grief passed through her which she was only just able to master.

It was a comforting spark for all that, and she swore by every god she had ever revered, by the great Spirit Who had made and ruled space, that she would not bring the helmet away with her or allow any of the others to do so. She was powerless to release Jake from his prison and tomb, but she would not let him die in the eternal blackness that was the true nature of this vile place.

TWENTY-TWO

ISLAEN CONNOR RECEIVED Bethe's findings quietly. Her head lowered and she turned away from her companions. Officers, particularly officers of the Commandos, had to expect to see comrades, close friends, die. They must bear it and go on with their work, but while they were expected to conduct themselves with strength and dignity, no one imagined they would be indifferent to their losses.

At least she was spared the choosing. She did not have to order that Jake Karmikel be abandoned to death so that they might continue their mission. With his body blocking the exit, they could not reach him without first going through the arsenal chamber that was their destination. Once they were finished there, they would have to work their way back, clear the blockage from the passage that had been their original route, and rappel down the rope again. Only they would arrive too late.

Varn Tarl Sogan had seen comrades he had loved go to their deaths and had sometimes given the command that had sent them into death, and he understood full well what his consort was suffering now. He had distanced himself from her during this crisis because she was their commander and it was important, for all of them, that she retain the cloak of strength and self-sufficiency. There could be no overt leaning upon him, not until it was over.

That constraint had not bound his thoughts, but he had held them aloof as well. He had remained locked behind his shields. The glimmering shade of an idea had come to him, and he had wanted to play it a while in secret lest he inflict the additional, uniquely acute anguish of forlorn hope on her if upon deeper consideration, it proved to be unworkable.

That did not seem to be the case. It was no plan he would normally have entertained, but it would work, or should, and his mind reached out now and touched gently with hers.

Do not despair yet, my Islaen. There is still a chance if Bandit will give us her help.

The gurry had been huddled miserably on a minute outcropping not far above the exit hole, silent and alone, as if she could not comprehend the tragedy that had descended so suddenly upon their company.

Her head lifted sharply at his words, and she instantly took wing. She whistled shrilly when she reached them, and he held out his hand to receive her.

He looked at her somberly. *There is possibly heavy peril in what I would have you do, and the certainty of harm to you.*

Bandit will do!

Very well, small one. I would not ask it if I thought we had any other choice. Listen to what we humans say. I will go over it again with you later in greater detail if you do not understand it all fully.

He glanced once at Islaen and received her nod, then snapped his head in the Hadesi's direction.

"Greggs, I read the equipment roster before we set out. You have a couple of spare lamps."

"Aye," he replied in surprise.

"Bring one here and take it apart. If we wrap the florase coils around that spire and then cut them, they should produce enough acid to eat through it."

"How can we do that, man? We can't reach the damn thing to attach them!"

"Bandit can."

"Bandit?"

He nodded. "According to Bethe's report, there is room for her to get through. Her bill is more than sharp enough to finish severing the coils if we begin the work for her."

"She can perform so complex a job?" Greggs asked doubtfully.

"She must. I shall be there to direct her through it."

Bethe Danlo straightened. "Let me—"

"I have to go, even apart from the need to work with Bandit. Some of that acid is bound to splash on Jake. The pain may well incapacitate him, and in that case it will be necessary to draw him out. You do not have the strength for that."

He caressed the gurry tenderly. "She will doubtless be affected as well."

Sogan recalled himself. "Have neutralizer ready and the renewer. There will be need for both."

The war prince hauled himself into the tunnel. Immediately a sick horror rushed upon him, but he quelled it impatiently. He had too much to do now to squander time or energy playing the coward.

"Small one," he whispered, "once you have cut the coils, go back to Islaen immediately, with all the speed you can. Do not wait to see what happens. Do you understand? She must neutralize whatever acid gets on you as soon as possible."

Bandit understands.

Would she obey? Would she be able to obey? "No matter how badly you are hurting, you must get to her."

I understand, Varn. She gave an excited, somewhat nervous-sounding whistle. *Jake's near! You tell him.*

"Aye, small one. I shall explain it all to him."

Karmikel's heart sank when he saw the Arcturian. They had failed, then. He concentrated on keeping his expression impassive and steeled himself to receive the now-expected confirmation of his doom.

Varn guessed the conclusion his coming in Bethe's stead must provoke in the trapped man and hastened to reassure him. He then explained the details of his plan.

The former Commando looked grim by the time he had finished but offered no protest. "I'll do just about anything to get out of here. I only wish Bandit didn't have to be involved."

"As do we all, but none of us could think of any other way.—Are you ready?"

"I am," he answered firmly, bracing himself as he spoke. "Tell her to go ahead."

The gurry took the partially severed coils from Sogan. She held them gingerly. If she did not altogether understand what would happen when the contents of the two thin tubes mingled, she had picked up enough of his respect for the reaction, of his fear of any accident and his fear for her, to treat her burden most carefully.

It was tricky work bringing the tubes to their target. She had room enough herself, but it was necessary to guard against tangling the coils or even jarring or scraping them against the wall or roof or against Jake's body, for fear of rupturing them prematurely.

Despite that care, it took her only a few minutes to reach the spire and less than half that time to twine the long coils around it, arranging them so the scored ends were in the lowest place.

Bandit hesitated at that point, remembering the Arcturian's statement that doing this thing would bring her pain; then she resolutely closed her beak sharply on each one in quick succession.

There was no avoiding picking up a minute amount of the liquids they contained. Her head snapped back as the acid formed and began its work. She fell and wildly began scraping her face and her bill on the stone floor.

"Bandit, fly!" Varn commanded with both mind and voice. "Take wing now! Go to Islaen!"

Somehow the gurry did get into the air again. She made her way back over Karmikel's body and Sogan's and picked up speed once she was clear of them. Shrieking in her agony, she streaked out of the tunnel.

She had not yet reached the entrance before the florase acid hit Jake. He screamed once but then clamped his jaws shut, although his body arched so violently as still more came down that his back struck hard against the low roof.

Varn's hands closed over his arms. "Hold, comrade. Hold on. The stone is almost burned through."

Would it go? Was there sufficient material in those coils to do it, or had too much of it dripped down and been wasted for its work to be accomplished?

The Arcturian's dark eyes fixed on the spire so intently that it seemed he would will it to shatter.

It was smoking along all its lower half. . . .

In the next moment it snapped and fell, still blackening and steaming, to lie in two pieces beside the man it had so very nearly slain.

It still might succeed. Karmikel's eyes were glazed, and if he were conscious at all, he was so enmeshed in pain and shock that he was incapable of rendering any assistance in his rescue.

Sogan tried to clear the sweat away from the other's eyes with the tips of his fingers. "Soon now, my friend. Islaen is waiting to receive you. She will give you ease."

He took hold of Jake's arms and began to drag him forward.

It was a titanic task, and several times Varn Tarl Sogan believed and feared it was one beyond his ability to accomplish, but always he willed himself to continue.

The smell of the acid itself and the worse odor of chemically burning flesh were powerful in that confined space. The fumes, which did concern him at first, were not sufficiently concentrated to overcome him, but his throat closed against them, so that he choked on each forced breath, and the combined stench made him feel deathly sick.

The war prince tried to clear all awareness of himself from his conscious mind. He needed to concentrate not only on maneuvering his own body through this viciously narrow hole—working almost blindly, since he had to depend for guidance upon brief glances taken over his shoulder when the roof raised high enough to permit him to lift himself that far—but he had to manipulate the heavy, inert form of his comrade as well. It was still all too possible for one or the other of them to become lodged again, perhaps permanently, more likely for a short space, but he feared that any delay whatsoever would prove fatal to Karmikel now. He was already in deep shock, maybe so deep that Islaen's ministrations would fail and this attempt would become no more than an exercise in clearing the tunnel for their return.

When he next looked back, Sogan saw light. It was strong enough to be visible despite the closer beams of his helmet and Jake's, both of which he was drawing along in the circle of his arms. He had gained the exit.

Moments later Larnse Greggs and Islaen were drawing him out. He let them take him until he had pulled the former Commando within their reach, then rolled aside to they could give Jake their complete attention.

TWENTY-THREE

VARN SAT BY the wall of the cave farthest from the accursed tunnel. His head was resting upon his arm and braced on his knees. His eyes were closed.

All the world seemed dim and hazy, his companions distant, unreal figures. His own body was weak and still wretchedly ill. He had tried to wield his will against himself as a lash, to force himself to rally, but that only seemed to reduce him still further, and he had given up the effort. He would just have to wait a while and hope he would come to himself again.

At least the others were occupied with the wounded. If luck were with him, none of them would notice him until he had recovered somewhat. He had no wish to disgrace himself before them. . . .

A steadying arm came around his shoulders.

Here, Varn, Islaen told him, *try to take some of this.*

He obediently swallowed a little of the contents of the tube she held for him. Recognizing the restorative, he forced himself to finish it.

The substance worked quickly, and after a few seconds Sogan raised his head. *Bandit? Karmikel?* he asked. It was an effort to speak even in thought, but at least he could.

Both fine now, but that acid's vile stuff. She made a face that drew the shadow of a smile from him. *I'm less happy than ever about carrying the makings of it about on my head.*

A whistle caused them both to look up. Bandit flew toward them and alighted on the Arcturian's knee.

Is Varn sick?

"Nothing like you were, small one," he told her, eyeing her critically. She seemed all right now, except that her bill looked a little ragged.

She should have more of the renewer, he told his consort.

Aye, but Jake's need is still the greater. We'll get to her as soon as we're done with him. She's in no pain now.

Once more he studied the small mammal, this time touching mind with her as well. A gurry might lie even as a human would in these circumstances.

"Is that so, little Bandit, or are you merely being valiant?"

Bandit's not brave. It hurt and hurt. Islaen fixed.

"I did not want that for you. Do you know that? In truth?"

Yes, the gurry replied calmly. *You wish it could've been you.* She took wing with that and returned to watch their companions work on Jake.

Sogan flushed, and Islaen laughed sympathetically.

I'm sorry, Varn, but your shields are in rather bad shape at the moment.

He colored again, this time in shame that he should be so reduced by mere effort while actual injuries had been taken and were in need of attention.

The former Admiral straightened so that he could better see the other three. He frowned, concern waking in him. Jake lay absolutely still, as if there were no life in him.

He looked sharply at Islaen. *How bad is he?*

He's all right, she assured him, *but he's had one foul time of it, and we've put him out. He won't be waking up for a good few hours.*

She took a towel from the first-aid kit he noticed for the first time and wiped off some of the icy sweat glistening on his face.

You could use some ministering to as well.

He shook his head. *I have no acid burns.*

Never mind the heroics, she told him sternly. *You might have escaped that part of it, but you've got a good case of florase poisoning, considerably worse than Jake's. You were working and pulled a lot more of the stuff into you.*

Florase poisoning, he muttered. *That explains a lot.* He scowled. *I should have realized we might be hit with it in there.*

Now don't go blaming yourself for something else! She softened suddenly. *I'm sorry to have been so long in coming to you.*

Karmikel needed you. I might not have realized about the florase, but I could see the state he was in.

Maybe, but you were so sick. You still are—

The war prince set his fingers to her lips and then let them brush softly against her cheek. *No apologies, Colonel. I lack the energy to battle them down at the moment.*

Islaen smiled. *Very well, Admiral.* She sighed. *I wish I could put you under oxygen, but as it is, you'll just have to sleep it off. You should be yourself in the morning.*

He nodded. A great weariness was taking hold of him, and he contented himself with watching her fish his blanket out of his pack. He would give her no argument about this.

Sogan slept like one dead for the next three hours, but dreams rose up to trouble him after that, dark, threatening shadows that eventually sent him back into full awareness.

He lay still for a few moments, breathing heavily. He could not remember now what had shocked him awake, or any of the images he had dreamed. He was grateful that he did not. There was enough to worry him in the waking world around him without calling up fancied perils as well.

The Arcturian tried to take stock of their present location, as much as he could without moving and perhaps disturbing his companions, and found little to comfort him in his discoveries. The cave was small. It was roughly circular, as many of them down here seemed to be, about twelve feet in diameter. The ceiling was only eight feet above them at most. Its closeness gave him an unpleasant feeling, as if they were taking their rest in a tomb, a vault meant to house only the dead.

He forced that analogy from his mind and closed his eyes. There was a stream nearby, probably the same one they had been following before reaching the crawlway. He could hear it plainly now, although he had not been aware of it earlier.

Varn felt no embarrassment over that failure. Florase poisoning fogged all the senses. He had done well enough, better than well, under the circumstances. He should have realized the potential when he had first considered his plan, but it would have made no difference in any event. He would still have gone ahead with it.

He felt a movement beside him and looked up, smiling as Islaen's mind touched his.

Do you ever sleep, Admiral? she asked him.

The same question might apply to you, Colonel Connor.

I've been busy.

She bent more closely over him, concern shadowing her large eyes. *Are you still having discomfort?*

No. I just had enough sleep, I suppose. He was not about to mention the matter of a few ill dreams.

She frowned. *You shouldn't. Not yet.* She lay her hand against his face. *You have no temperature anyway.*

Varn sat up. *I am fine now. The gas is out of my system.*

He looked at her sharply. Her face was white and pinched with weariness, and she still carried the shadow of worry.

What has been going on, Islaen? You have not even un-rolled your blanket. What else has happened in this demon-blighted hole?

Nothing. Take it easy, will you? Bethe and I have been keeping an eye on you and Jake, that's all. You were both restless enough to worry us a bit.

How is Karmikel?

Doing well now. Her face clouded. *He was fevered for a while. We were afraid he might be going sour on us, but it was just a reaction to it all.*

Her eyes fixed pensively on him, and he felt her love for him swell suddenly and so powerfully that he started in amazement. *My Islaen—*

Your fear for him, your care, were as strong as my own.

His eyes fell. *Karmikel is my comrade, Islaen, my friend. If some weakness of mine makes me see him as a sort of rival as well, that counts as nothing. If I should ever slink down to that—*

Never could you, his consort replied quickly and with a passionate certainty as deep as her own soul.

He said nothing. His consciousness of her glory was too overwhelming, that and his wonder that he had won this confidence, this feeling, from her.

I should not so fail you, Islaen Connor, he whispered almost fiercely.

The emotion on him made him even more aware of her weariness. He studied her tenderly and with no little sense of shame. She had not spared herself throughout all the day just past, and still she had kept watch over him. . . .

He frowned. Maybe more than that. There were what appeared to be fresh stains on her jacket and a smear of damp red dirt on her forehead, which he was nearly certain had not been there when he had last spoken with her. If one like it had been there, the stream was right here at hand. She would have washed it away long since.

You have been back in the tunnel. Recently. Why?

He did not like to think of her in that place, and his question was sharper than he had intended.

She gave no indication of surprise or annoyance but merely let her fingers brush against his. *Someone had to clear it out, Varn. The rock itself might cause us problems on our return, and I was afraid to leave whatever was left of the acid in there. I waited until the gas had time to dissipate and crawled in with the neutralizer.*

Why you? he demanded.

Who else was there? You and Jake were out of it, and Bethe had certainly done her share and more already.

Greggs—He stopped. He would not have trusted the Hadesi to do anything that he could do himself. Islaen must have felt the same way.

Sorry, I was not thinking.

On the contrary, I fear. You've been thinking too much and have started getting protective of your own.

The lightness of her tone took the sting out of her remark, and he did not rise to it.

You could be right there, he admitted.

Of course I'm right.—Varn, would you please go back to sleep? I'm bone tired, but if you don't rest as well, I'll be too worried about you to close an eye.

Now who is becoming protective? Sogan smiled and lay back. *Very well, Colonel. I shall do my best to accommodate you.*

TWENTY-FOUR

It was Islaen's laughter that woke the Arcturian—happy, free laughter such as he had not imagined ever to hear in this eternally dark maze.

He sat up quickly. What did Hades' underworld contain that could spark it?

His companions were all crouched on the bank of the stream. They were peering intently into it, unaware of him.

What is going on?

Come see, she responded eagerly. *These make up for those beetles and triwings!*

Wildlife. He might have guessed, he thought as he got to his feet. Islaen responded positively and strongly to an enormous spectrum of nonhuman creatures, and Hades of Persephone would have to be poor indeed to support nothing capable of arousing her enthusiasm.

Joining the others, he saw that the water was quite clear, and he immediately spotted the creatures. Although he did not kneel beside her, a smile softened his face. There were an even dozen of them, swimming things he at first took to be fish, until he recalled Hades had given rise to none. Reptiles, probably, he decided, or some very advanced insect.

They were two inches in length and about an eighth of an inch thick, all save the heads. They had no fins or limbs but moved by undulating their albino bodies in a quick, graceful fashion. The heads were comparatively huge, eyeless, of course, and split by enormous mouths set permanently in a foolish-looking smile.

The effect of this last was intensified as they fed, he saw, as he watched two of them seize some of the crumbs Islaen was dropping into the water.

"Just like self-satisfied gurries," he remarked, laughing softly to himself.

Bandit, who was with the Commando as usual, gave an angry squawk. *Not gurries!*

No, he agreed hastily. *Do not excite yourself. Your kind is unique in both ultrasystems.*

Yes!

"Is this wise?" he asked aloud. "Could there be danger in giving them our food?"

"None," Larnse Greggs assured him. "As I've already explained to Colonel Connor, they are gathering even now in anticipation of the feast of relatively strange items the approaching seasonal rains will soon begin sending into the caves. It's during these next four months that mating, laying, and hatching take place down here. In fact, many creatures gather just about all their food now and hibernate for most of the rest of the year."

Jake looked up, his eyes narrowing slightly. "What's the chance of flooding?"

"None in this system. Excess water is shunted off before it reaches here. Ribonets like a relatively stable environment and are never found in flood-prone streams."

The former Commando nodded but felt he had another sound reason to be glad when the time came to leave Hades' underworld.

Islaen had been through that discussion already and barely heard it now. Her attention was held by the little Hadesi swimmers.

Varn's eyes were on her rather than on them. He loved to watch her in moments like this.

A sudden darkness swept into his mind, crushing his spirit as a roof fall would crush out his life. He managed to block its transmission and turned hastily away before she could sense there was trouble on him. They had known little pleasure these last days. Let her enjoy these few moments of it before she had to take up the burden of responsibility and heavy purpose again.

His head lifted. His own decision must come later. Until

then, this remained his to bear. He would not allow it to add to the pressures Islaen Connor already had to carry.

His estimation that the interlude would be a short one proved accurate. She regretfully came to her feet only a couple of minutes later.

"We had best eat now ourselves and then go on."

She gazed none too happily at the place where the stream disappeared into the cave wall. "I suppose that's our exit, since I don't see any other."

"It is," Greggs admitted.

"We have to swim?" Jake Karmikel demanded. "How much headroom will we have? There's none at all at the wall."

"It's a sump, completely filled. We'll only be a minute and a half passing through it, two minutes if you're nervous and want to go slow."

"You might have mentioned this in the beginning!"

The Hadesi scowled. "I never thought to say anything," he said defensively. "You don't have to know how to swim. You can pull yourselves along, and anyone picked for this job would have to have the control and be in good enough condition to be able to hold his breath for a couple of minutes."

"You mentioned a second tight passage," Sogan said quietly. "Is this it?"

He nodded. "Aye. There's a forest of stalactites growing from the roof, ready to trap any swimmer. We'll have to partially strip to get through. Our trousers fit tightly enough not to cause trouble, but we will have to remove all clothing from our upper bodies or we won't have a hope of making it to the other side without at least one of us getting caught. Outside of that, though, there should be no real problem beyond a little discomfort. The water's cold."

"I thought the Resistance used this route," Jake said.

"We did. Every mission conducted by the Karst cell was supplied through it."

"Then why in the name of space didn't you just snap those dragon's teeth?"

The guide drew himself up with a dignity they had not seen on him before. "We were fighting for Hades. We were not about to mutilate her ourselves."

Karmikel was quiet only a moment. "You have my apologies, Greggs. Few other populations, maybe no other, had that kind of strength.''

Larnse nodded, accepting both the apology and the compliment to his kind. He eyed the off-worlders' packs with some envy. ''You may fare better than me in this. Those look to be waterproof.''

''They are,'' Islaen agreed. ''Commando issue. There's room enough in mine to take your shirt and jacket.''

He started to thank her but stopped in alarm as another thought struck him. ''What about your gurry? She might suffocate if you put her in the pack, but there's no headroom at all for her to fly through.''

''Bandit can swim, at least with me to help push her along.''

She stroked the little hen, as if pondering. *Can you do it, love, hold your breath so long? Would you rather I put you in the pack?*

Bandit will swim. She gave a shrill whistle. *Bandit said we should have gone to Jade.*

Islaen smiled, but her eyes were fixed on Sogan. There was a challenge to be met before they ever began their swim, maybe a deadly one for him.

The Arcturian had withdrawn as far as the confines of the cave would permit and was staring in seeming anger at the place where the stream was exiting into the sump. He had not anticipated this turn of events.

We have no choice, Varn.

I know.

Admiral Varn Tarl Sogan's story was known throughout the Federation, but belief in his death under the lashes of his own people was an unquestioned part of it. They would just have to hope that neither Bethe Danlo nor Greggs would make the connection and realize he had survived the execution of the sentence the Empire's court-martial had set on him. At least the scarring was not now so terribly awesome as to instantly identify him, although, the Spirit of Space knew, it was still bad enough.

Come back to us, she instructed quickly. *Act naturally. You can't hide those scars now, and if you try, you'll only call more attention to them.*

The war prince straightened without answering her and

went to where he had left his pack. He knelt, opened it, and swiftly removed both his jacket and tunic, positioning himself so his back was toward the others, as if he gave no thought to it.

Jake stiffened. He had to fight to keep his hands from shaking.

He had known the renewer treatment had resulted in only partial cosmetic improvement, but Islaen had said it was significant all the same and had declared that both she and Sogan were well satisfied. What had those original injuries been like that this could be regarded as any sort of success at all?

Larnse Greggs was kneeling beside him, checking that the perishables in his own pack were indeed properly water-proofed. He looked almost green.

"Who did that to him?" he whispered. He had seen similar work, although always freshly done and never before on a living man.

"Arcturians," Karmikel hissed savagely. "Now just shut up. He doesn't like to be reminded of it."

Varn finished sealing his pack and stood once more, grate-fully turning his back away from eyes that felt like knives boring into it.

The response? he asked stiffly.

Shock.—I think we're all right. Courtesy will keep them away from us down here, and I don't think either Bethe or Greggs is the type to shoot off his mouth when we get to the surface again. Just keep on playing it like you are.

Jake Karmikel was standing beside Bethe, both to help her and because he wanted to give the other two a chance to be alone for a few minutes. It was not hard to imagine how uncomfortable Sogan must be feeling.

The demolitions expert waited until Larnse disappeared into the sump before turning to her companion. "Why?" she questioned in a barely audible whisper. "Why would they do that to one of their own?"

He hesitated, but she knew or had surmised so much already that he went on.

"Mercy can be costly. He refused to destroy without purpose."

Bethe only nodded, then suddenly her breath came in a quick gasp and her hand rose to cover her mouth.

"Thorne . . ." Her eyes closed. "By the great Spirit ruling space, I should have known. He's even almost kept his name."

"He was too far out of it when he was rescued to make one up." The redhead turned to her desperately. "Bethe, please . . ."

Her eyes flashed. "Do you imagine I would betray that man? Do you think so little of me?"

"Thanks, friend.—Greggs should be through by now."

"He said to give him five minutes," she replied, her voice tight. The thought of finding a dead body blocking her way when she dived was not an appealing one.

Bethe put that from her mind and slid into the stream without any outward hesitation when the specified time was past. She gasped as the cold water struck her skin, then took a deep breath and dove into the sump.

It was eerie in that drowned passage, so strange that she might have entered into another state of being entirely, a realm of odd buoyancy and weirdly shimmering light.

There was no overlooking the stalactites. Jake had termed them dragon's teeth, and so they were, precisely like the great fangs of some of Fairie's most deadly denizens. It was a squeeze to get under some of them, not impossible by any means even for one much larger than herself, but any tunic, not to mention a shirt or a jacket, would have provided enough loose material for snagging, becoming a distinct peril.

She seemed to be underwater for a long time, and her lungs were calling for release. Something must have gone wrong. . . .

Another light, shining down into the water!

Beth broke surface. She drew in a lungful of air and gratefully allowed Larnse to help her onto the bank.

She was not long in dressing. She was chilled to the bone after that swim and took no pleasure in displaying herself before anyone. Spacers traveled for long periods of time in very close quarters, and their kind had learned long since—so long that it was now instinct with them—to dress and conduct themselves in a way that worked to minimize the tensions inevitable to such voyaging.

At least her body was no embarrassment to her, she thought

ruefully as she slipped her jacket on. Her form was a good one by any Terran-type standard.

She shook her head, annoyed with herself, and hastened to help Islaen, who had just broken water at nearly the same spot she had surfaced.

Sogan came through next. The Colonel went to give him her hand, leaving the still waterlogged Bandit to lick herself dry in peace beneath Bethe's jacket.

The spacer stroked the little creature, warming and comforting her, but her attention was fixed on Islaen Connor.

For nearly the whole course of their time together, she had wondered how any woman could have turned from Jake Karmikel for this former enemy of theirs, but now, knowing the kind of man Varn Tarl Sogan was and must have been, she understood, although she did not believe she would have made the same choice as Islaen. She doubted she would have had the courage, the inner strength, to do so.

Bethe regarded the lovely Commando with awe. What must it be to take what could only be a desperately wounded man like this to oneself? Islaen must have to constantly be on the alert, about herself, her words, her gestures, even her silences. . . .

Jake's arrival scattered her thoughts. She waved to the other two, indicating that she would meet him, and bent to steady him as he climbed out onto the bank.

She retrieved his pack for him, but when she bent again to open it, she was stopped by an annoyed whistle. A pocket of damp warmth moved under her shirt, and a moment later Bandit emerged from beneath the garment, looking ruffled and obviously displeased.

The spacer laughed. "Sorry, pet. I guess I was moving around too much. Why not go back to your friends now?—Go on. Go to Islaen!"

She laughed again as she watched the gurry obey and turned shamefacedly to Jake. "You'd think she understood every word I was saying, the way I was talking to her for a minute there."

"Everyone treats gurries like that," he replied, his eyes sparkling. "Look there," he added as the Arcturian raised his hand to receive the Jadite creature. "Even Sogan fusses over

her, which is more than he does with Islaen.'' He grinned.
''Publicly at least.''

''You just keep quiet and let them be, Jake Karmikel,'' the
spacer warned somewhat sharply.

He lifted his brows. ''Getting protective, aren't you?''

''Never mind, you blackguard. I'm thinking those two
deserve a bit of peace.''

Once Jake had finished dressing, they joined their other
comrades.

The Colonel immediately turned to Larnse Greggs. ''I
believe we're all ready now,'' she told him. ''I see what
appear to be two potential routes.''

''We take the larger. It's a climb. We'll have to chimney
up it, in fact.—You all know what that means?'' he asked in
an afterthought. Thus far the Federation party had performed
so well and with such obvious grasp of at least the basics of
cave travel that he had forgotten for a moment that what was
to him a perfectly commonplace term might be unrecognized
by these others.

All of them nodded, although none with any show of
enthusiasm.

''How long is the climb?'' Islaen asked him.

''Thirty-three feet.''

The Hadesi looked speculatively at Bethe. ''I'm glad you're
no shorter. The chimney widens a bit at its center, but I think
you can make it. If you find you cannot, or fear you cannot,
go back down. We'll lower a rope for you.''

''Wouldn't it have been easier just to stick one in there in
the first place, like at the big pit?'' she inquired.

He shook his head. ''We didn't dare, not so close to the
arsenal. It would've been like a map to the Arcturians if they
ever reached this point, either to our arms or backward along
the course to it. Besides, we don't need one. Hadesim spend
as much time underground as on the surface, and we find the
methods of moving around down here as easy as those you
space hounds use to get about the innards of a starship.''

''I hadn't thought of it that way,'' Bethe admitted.

She stepped back while Jake and Islaen examined the
chimney. Their mountain training would stand them in good
stead now. It might help them determine if there were some

reason why the party should not attempt this passage, and it would provide useful information about the climb ahead.

She wouldn't mind if they could ease the way a little, she thought. She was blessed with a good imagination, and the idea of climbing that narrow tube with her back braced against one wall while her feet walked up the opposite wall was both vivid and unappealing.

Bethe felt a movement and turned to see Varn Tarl Sogan standing beside her.

"You will do fine," he told her softly. "You have proven yourself exceedingly capable thus far, and anyone who can maneuver and function in a ship's drive tubes can manage this."

She gave him a grateful smile. "Thanks. I can use the vote of confidence just now."

"You have earned it.—Do not fear. We are resuming our old line of march. I shall go up ahead of you and will handle the ropes if you should call for them." A surprisingly warm smile flickered for a moment in his eyes and on his lips. "Those, too, a space hound knows how to use."

Sogan hauled himself onto the benchlike ledge from which he would begin his ascent and looked up the chimney, trying to gauge the difficulty of the climb from what he could observe of it.

He saw Islaen Connor lean over from the top, which she and Greggs had already attained. He smiled and raised his hand in a half salute.

It was not bravado. The Arcturian did not fear this ascent. He knew his body was capable of it. The work would be hard, but barring some ill throw of chance, he should have no trouble with it.

He set his back to the wall behind him and rammed his feet firmly into the one facing him. He would literally walk up the chimney, using the relatively broad expanse of his back to brace him and to break his descent if he should slip.

Sogan slowly worked his way up the wall, wincing whenever he came into contact with an exceptionally large or sharp projection but not hesitating or suffering any mishap. It was not comforting to recognize that the threat posed by a fall increased with every inch he gained, but he felt little concern.

Almost from the beginning he had realized this was no great
challenge either to his strength or his will.

His mood darkened as he reached the centerpoint of the
climb. The walls drew apart, as Greggs had said they would.
Varn frowned as his legs straightened to follow them. Islaen
had made it before him, and he would have even less of a
problem, but he worried about Bethe Danlo. She was much
shorter than the Commando, and he wondered if Greggs
might not have underestimated the extent of her reach. He
need have been only a little off for the ascent to be impossible
for her.

He went no more than a few feet before he felt the walls
drawing together again.

Sogan glanced up. Islaen was still there, waiting for him.
He increased his pace the little he dared, until he was able to
pull himself onto a level with her. Once he reached that point,
both she and Larnse Greggs helped draw him into the corridor
that was their destination.

He had his balance in the next moment, and they all knelt
to watch the spacer begin her ascent.

"She's game," the Commando remarked aloud as Bethe
started working her way up toward them.

"Not too much so, I hope," he replied.

"To the point of folly? Not that one."

The Arcturian frowned. *Jake is standing directly beneath
her.*

Islaen gave him an amused glance. *Of course. The distance
is such that a body's fall might well be cushioned by another.
You positioned yourself so when I was climbing.*

He quickly turned his gaze below. *Karmikel was a Commando. He still is, for all practical purposes.*

His consort managed not to smile either in mind or with her
lips. It was not often that the war prince set his caste in a
lesser place with respect to any other group, even his elite
former enemies.

*He's no key member of this mission and so can afford to be
freer in risking himself, especially since Bethe Danlo happens
to be the pivotal figure of our little group.*

Varn did not reply. Bethe was approaching the place where
the chimney bulged outward now, and all three of them
tensed.

Larnse's lips tightened when he saw her legs straighten. "I'd best get the rope ready," he said. "She's only at the approach."

"Aye . . ." Islaen began. "No. Hold up. She'll make it, I think."

The next few moments would tell whether the demolitions expert would be able to complete the climb or be forced to retreat and wait for her comrades to haul her up. Her face contorted for an instant as she stretched her body to the point of real pain, but then she was over the worst spot and was climbing steadily once more.

A short while later she came within reach of her comrades. With them to steady and help lift her, the rest was easy, and she was soon standing amongst them, leaning heavily on Sogan until her breath returned to its normal rate.

At last she took on her own weight once more. "Some mission," the spacer grumbled. "Every muscle in my body is either stretched into a string, squashed into microcircuit size, or tied in a knot."

As if to give the lie to her words, she dropped to her knees and glided to the edge of the chimney to watch Jake Karmikel make his climb.

The former Commando came up no more quickly than any of his companions, but his strength and size made it a relatively simple exercise for him, and his highland training, though taken years before, gave him a confidence, a smoothness and self-assurance in his movements, that Sogan knew he had not come near matching.

The Noreenan man was scarcely up before he fixed his eyes on the Colonel. She nodded. The same question was burning in all the off-worlders' minds.

"Greggs, you indicated below that this place is near the arsenal. How near?"

"Within half an hour's fast walk, Colonel Connor. No more than that."

TWENTY-FIVE

ISLAEN CONNOR FELT herself tighten as she always did when battle was imminent. Varn tensed as well, as did the other two off-worlders. They were relieved, right enough, that the end of their mission was in sight, but the sense of potential danger, the inner preparation for combat, were the paramount emotions in all of them now. No one had forgotten that dead spacer or the fact that his comrades were here in these tunnels along with them.

Islaen permitted herself to display none of the agitation or excitement within her. "What kind of terrain will we encounter?" she inquired of the Hadesi.

"Like you see here. The floor is very uneven, and there are a number of deep holes, some of them well camouflaged until you're right on them, so we'll have to watch where we put our feet. Otherwise, it's a clear walk. We take the left corridor."

She swept the tunnel with her light for the full length its beam would reach. As Greggs indicated, the floor was very littered and broken, but the passage itself was huge in comparison with most of those they had encountered thus far, easily large enough to admit her flier. At least this section of it was.

"Does it run straight the whole way?" she asked.

"Not at all. There are numerous twists, but the corridor's so big that we'll hardly notice them except as a change of scenery." He could anticipate her next questions, and added, "We won't have to worry about terrain during our approach to the arsenal, nor do we have to concern ourselves about any

168

reasonable noise we might make. The acoustics of the tunnel
and cave are such that low sounds, including quiet speech,
can't pass from one to the other in either direction. We can't
let off any charges, of course, but as long as we're cautious,
we won't tip anyone off that we're coming, even if the pirates
are already inside.''

"Just as they won't give us any warning of their presence?''

He nodded. "I'm afraid so. Luckily, our entrance provides
an excellent vantage to spy the situation out, better than we
would've had on our original course, actually.''

"What about sentries? It'll be hard avoiding them in this
passage.''

"They won't have any outside the chamber itself.''

Jake Karmikel flashed him a sharp look. "That's a strange
setup for a Resistance hold,'' he drawled, and the two who
had served with him before recognized the threat in his
seemingly quiet tone.

"We never used it without ample guards,'' Larnse agreed,
"and there'll be sentries now if Geord does have a part in
this, but they'll all be inside. I'm nearly certain of that.''

"What's the good of them, then?'' the redhead demanded.

"No one can get through either entrance if an alert guard's
holding it, and don't forget, they have no reason to expect
trouble. Even if they did, I doubt you could get any of that
off-world scum to take a lone post out here in these tunnels.''

He is right there, Varn said slowly to Islaen. *I would not
want to do it unless there were strong cause to drive me, and
I do not think I flatter myself overmuch in believing I am
better disciplined than curs from any wolf pack.*

*Better disciplined, and you wouldn't have the nagging fear
that maybe your comrades might just quietly slip off and leave
you standing here. Pirates and those of their ilk are known
to take some pretty sharp measures to settle their grudges.*

Her eyes flickered back to Greggs. "You are certain they
cannot be attacked if they're in there and reasonably on the
alert?''

"Nothing's absolutely certain, Colonel. That's why we of
the Resistance kept up a good guard whenever we came down
here, but an assault wouldn't be easy, not even for a company
more elaborately armed than ours. The passage itself is wide,
but the entrance to the arsenal's a narrow slit that will admit

only one person at a time. It leads out onto a slender outcropping far enough off the floor—seven feet on its lower side,
eight on the higher—that anyone dropping from it must first
recover his balance and orient himself again before using any
weapon. He'd be cut down before he could defend himself,
much less fight.''

"Drop the sentries from the ledge itself?"

He shook his head. "Anyone stepping out onto it is immediately visible, a target for every blaster in the chamber
below, and, again, he would not be ready to fire immediately
himself. The delay isn't long, but it's necessary to squeeze
through the entrance crevice, making instantaneous battle
impossible."

"What about firing through the slit?" Bethe inquired. "You
say we can see them through it."

"Geord'll have his sentries placed so they're out of line of
any such fire," he replied contemptuously, "and the planetbuster's set well away from it as well. You can forget that
one unless some of you are carrying heavier arms than I
imagine."

There was a trace of hope in that last, but Islaen Connor
shook her head. "Gear like that was never normal issue for
us, and this wasn't expected to be a problem mission. We'll
have to manage with conventional small antipersonnel weapons."

Her head lowered as she thought for several seconds. Then
she looked up again. "The other party may be gone, making
all this unnecessary, but the timing is such that we're more
likely to find them in possession of the arsenal. We won't
know what the situation is or what we can do about it until we
have a real look at the place.

"We'll continue on together a while longer, until we've
covered half the remaining distance, then Greggs and I will
go on alone."

Bethe Danlo took a step forward. "I go with you.—That
planetbuster's my job, Colonel. It's important, and possibly
imperative, that I get a look at it as soon as possible, particularly if anyone's been messing with it."

Islaen did not hesitate before nodding her assent. "Very
well. You come, but I don't want to hear from any other

volunteers," she added to silence their two comrades, both of whom were about to protest their own passive roles.

They set off in the direction Greggs had indicated, moving silently, on the alert for sign of their enemies despite the guide's declaration that they would find none. Larnse himself was watching as carefully as any of the others.

Varn Tarl Sogan matched his pace with that of his consort. *Watch well, Islaen. I do not like your going on ahead with him. If he has any idea of—*

He doesn't. There's no feel of treachery at all about him. —I'll stay linked with you and open my receptors into yours. You'll see everything I do and can give Jake a running account.

He nodded. *That will have to suffice for us. Just do not take any needless chances.*

She smiled. *Do you imagine I would?*

Aye, Commando, he replied grimly, *chances that I would term needless.*

Islaen Connor cut her lamp, and after allowing her eyes a few seconds to adjust to the onslaught of darkness, she began to creep forward over the ground she had spied out minutes before. Eventually she reached the solid, cold wall separating the tunnel from the cave beyond. Half feeling her way along it, she was quick to locate the entrance slit.

It looked to be a tight squeeze at its farther lip, but she did not attempt to slip through it. She could see well enough from within to suit her purpose for the moment.

The arsenal was a large, irregularly shaped chamber, and also quite a beautiful one. Flowstone sheathed the walls in many places, and floor and ceilings supported a number of stalagmites and stalactites. All but a couple of these were small to middle size, and no columns had as yet formed. Many were very attractively shaded.

There were numerous signs of the purpose this place had served. Other, more urgent work had taken priority over clearing out such depots, and a large number of empty boxes and crates still lay as they had been left when the Resistance had removed their contents for use against the invaders. Most of those that had been untouched at the War's end had been taken out in response to this new threat, and only one of all the deadly things once housed here now remained—a squat, graceless-looking cylinder sitting nearly in the center of the cave, just out of direct line of her vantage point.

She had more than sufficient light to study it, light cast by nine strong lamps. The other party had reached the chamber before them and was now in full possession of it.

The Commando's face was bleak as she studied her opponents. Not one, but a pair, guarded each of the two entrances and were so placed that even if an attacker succeeded in forcing an entry and dropped one sentry, the other would remain to burn him down. The other five were clustered around the huge form of the planetbuster, watching while one of their company worked on it, apparently in an attempt to pry out the plate covering its sensitive brain mechanism in preparation for dismantling the missile. He seemed not to be enjoying much success, and the readings she was picking up were heavy with frustration and impatience.

A study of the individuals comprising the party told her enough about them to identify what they were.

One of the sentries posted nearest her was a Hadesi to judge by his appearance and clothes. The others were offworlders, spacers, five obviously male, the rest either women or striplings of either sex, probably the former, judging by size and build. All of them seemed to be a hard lot, scum of the type Navy and Patrol alike were sworn to exterminate.

Of more immediate significance, all were well and heavily armed, and there was no doubt at all in her mind that they had both the skill and the willingness to use those weapons, and with little provocation.

She carefully retreated to where the other two scouts were waiting and motioned for Bethe Danlo to take her turn at the vantage point. She would be the last. Greggs had gone up first.

Islaen felt the demolitions expert's tension, the trace of excitement, as she maneuvered herself into position. A surge of alarm overrode all other emotion. Almost immediately it fell to a manageable level, but it remained a solid core of concern radiating from the spacer.

To Islaen's relief, Bethe returned quickly and gave the signal to start back down the corridor. They moved swiftly and in silence, not stopping again until they had reached the off-world men.

In order to preserve the secret of her mental contact with Sogan, Islaen had to recount what she had seen in the arsenal, although she had already shared that information with them. It was not a wasted effort, at least, for by putting her observations into words, she had to organize and clarify them in her own mind.

"If we get into that cave, we should be able to take them," she declared at the end of her report. "They have the advantage in numbers, but the two guarding the farther entrance can be discounted for the first crucial seconds, and if the others remain bunched as they are—and there's no reason to assume they won't, under the circumstances—then we'd be able to take out at least a couple more there fairly quickly. After that we'd have to fight, but these are pirates, not guerrillas, and this isn't their style of warfare."

"If we get in," Jake repeated. "That seems to be the rub, doesn't it?"

"We'll jolly well have to get in, and fast," Bethe Danlo told him grimly. "They've started working on the planetbuster, and they're doing it all wrong. It's a near miracle they haven't blown all this quadrant of Hades to bits already, and us with it, and we don't have a whole lot of time left before they do just that. On the current models you have to detach the entire—"

She stopped. The Hadesi, at least, would not understand a highly technical description, nor was one necessary here.

"The brain's in more or less the same spot in both versions, but to disassemble the modern ones, you just pull out the entire unit and cart it off as a whole. That's what they imagine's under the panel they're trying to unfasten at the moment. However, on these antiques only the small center square should be removed. Otherwise the thing's automatically activated. Luckily, the years and the damp must've made the seals stubborn, or we'd be dust already, but I doubt they'll hold much longer."

Her eyes had the look of solar steel. "Even if they do, all the hammering may start it up anyway. Those things were pulled and redesigned specifically because they had the tendency to turn on at inconvenient moments, like after getting a good jolt, say during the course of a battle.''

"Nice," the redhead muttered. "And our entrance is bad, Islaen?''

She nodded. "Greggs called it. The corridor extends into the cave as a blunt tongue, three feet or so long, one wide. The drop looks to be seven feet to the right, eight to the left. We can do it, but we won't come down blasting. There would have to be a few moments' recovery time, and the guards'll have anyone trying it fried before half that's over.''

She frowned. "Someone lying prone on the ledge could cover the penetration man long enough for him to recover and give protection in turn. After that we'd be away with it, but I doubt we can get a second person through that crevice fast enough. It's awfully narrow.''

"It would be possible if those below could be distracted, their responses frozen, for a couple of seconds?'' the former Admiral asked.

"Aye.''

Larnse shook his head emphatically. "If you're thinking of shouting or setting off some sort of explosion, forget it. Geord is with them, right enough, and he won't fall for that. He's one of the sharpest men I've ever met.''

"I had something else in mind," Varn Tarl Sogan told him. "Does your kinsman—''

"I have no kin!''

The other man lowered his head in acknowledgment. "Does this renegade speak Arcturian?''

Greggs stared in surprise. "Aye. Of course. All of us who fought them spoke it fluently.'' He glowered. "That means just about the whole population, infants excluded, space hound.''

Varn seemed not to hear the Hadesi. "It was thus on Thorne as well,'' he murmured more to himself than to any of his companions. "The pirates are likely to have a few phrases as well, enough to serve our needs.''

Islaen's great eyes bore into him. "What are you getting at?''

"If I slip out on that tongue without light, I should gain just enough time to provide the necessary diversion. Even if I am burned down myself, my follow-up will have time to drop the sentries. The attack can proceed as we would have after that.''

Larnse Greggs looked at the Federation man with a kind of respect, his pale eyes glowing. ''It'd be risky, but it just might work,'' he said softly.

The Colonel offered no protest with mind or voice, although her heart felt cold within her. They had little other choice with time itself against them.

''I'll come after you. I'm smaller than either Greggs or Jake and will be able to get through the crevice that much faster.''

''I'm smallest of all,'' Bethe reminded her.

''You're to stay out of this,'' Islaen told her flatly. ''If you get yourself killed, all the rest is pretty pointless.—That goes for you too,'' she told the gurry, whose fully extended plumage declared that she was readying herself for the fast-approaching confrontation.

Islaen caught herself. ''You'll have to hold her when we move out, Bethe.''

The spacer nodded. ''I'll wait at the entrance, though. I want to get to work fast once you've cleared out that slime.''

''That was to be my next order.''

Bethe reached for Bandit, but the gurry took wing and eluded her.

Nooo! Bandit will go!

You will obey your orders, the Arcturian snapped. *You have no power over hate or violence of this magnitude and would only give us further cause for worry.*

The hen stopped in midair, stunned. Varn had never commanded her in this manner before, had never spoken harshly to her, but she returned meekly to Islaen's shoulder and allowed the demolitions expert to catch hold of her. She knew by then that she could not soften a great many of humanity's more violent passions once they took full hold, and she could read the fear her two humans already felt for one another. She would not put concern for her on them as well.

Thanks, Varn, Islaen said, then immediately returned to the upcoming battle.

''Greggs, you'll have to play it as it comes. I'd prefer to hold you as a backup and as a guard against any of them getting out this way, but if we're having it rough, you might judge it wiser to give us a hand.''

"Fair enough, Colonel.''

There was little more to say, and they started up the tunnel. In a few moments they would be at the arsenal. Shortly after that they would be in battle.

Varn Tarl Sogan walked beside the Commando. Neither said anything. Their thoughts were now tightly shielded, although their minds were still lightly linked. That contact, too, would soon be severed, not to be resumed until the conflict was ended.

Maybe it would never be resumed. Now that it was almost upon them, it seemed impossible to him that they should both survive the risks inherent in the first few minutes of the assault.

A chill deep as that pervading space gripped Sogan, and he turned his head slightly to look upon the Noreenan woman.

She was exquisite. Even these last, hard days underground could not diminish her loveliness, but it was not her beauty he saw now. He was watching Islaen Connor herself, this woman who had given him life in the place of a bleak and worthless existence, this woman who was his life to an extent he did not dare acknowledge even to himself. It was inconceivable to imagine that in a short while nothing might remain of her save a lifeless, mutilated shell.

The Arcturian forced himself to face that possibility, but he raised no protest against her involvement. That was no more possible for him than it had been possible for her to argue against the role he had chosen to assume. They had no other choice if the danger the pirates posed was to be lifted from Hades of Persephone. The responsibility was theirs, and if the threat of death hung heavily over them as a result, that was but theirs to accept. Danger was part of the lifeway they had chosen to make their own.

Peril to himself he did accept, nor was he troubled overly much by it. He did not court death, especially not now, but he did not tremble before the possible ending of his life, particularly in clean battle, in a manner acceptable to his kind. It might too readily have come otherwise. By any stretch of reason, he should have been slaughtered years ago, and more than he could have expected, he had been favored since then. The Empire's gods were harsh, and they did not readily allow a man to rebuild his life once it had been broken.

Islaen Connor had wrought that miracle for him, but now he turned away from her physically and in mind and fixed his gaze on the red stone of the passage ahead of them. Dwelling any further on the specter of her destruction would serve only to weaken him and, indeed, was a violation of his duty. Only a few minutes remained to them before they would have to go into action. Instead of squandering his time nurturing dread of a disaster which might or might not come to pass and which he was powerless to alter if it did, he would do better to refine his plans, such as they were, and develop alternate courses, should his original ideas prove impracticable.

TWENTY-SIX

FAR TOO QUICKLY for Sogan the Federation unit reached the place from which they would begin their attack.

The Arcturian first dimmed and then cut his lamp entirely. Taking infinite care lest he stumble and perhaps make some noise audible to their enemies despite Greggs' assurances about the tunnel's acoustics he crept forward, using the little light seeping in from the chamber beyond to guide him.

When he reached the entrance, he paused awhile, studying the scene before him.

It was more or less unchanged from the way Islaen's receptors had shown it, but he was seeking specific detail now, detail around which to finalize his plan—or force him to alter or abandon it entirely.

His lips compressed into a hard, unpleasant line.

As the Commando had noted, the renegade Hadesi was holding watch on the right-hand side of the stone outcropping. He was alert, attending to his work, in contrast to the more relaxed attitude of his companion on the left. It would be no easy matter accomplishing his will against that one.

He had hoped the fact that he was going in dark would be enough to cover him, making the more dangerous ruse unnecessary, but he realized almost at once that it would not be possible. There was still too much light. He would not step forth as a beacon, as would have been the case if his own lamp were activated, but the Hadesi would be quick to spot him all the same. He would have, perhaps, fifteen seconds, no more.

It was not sufficient. That renegade must be distracted,

paralyzed, if just for a few moments, or he was a dead man and his comrades' hopes of a victory were dead along with him.

Sogan felt Islaen move into place behind him. He took a deep breath and held it a moment to steady himself, then exhaled to make himself as small as possible as he crept through the crevice joining the armory with the tunnel system through which they had come.

Even as he tensed to make the drop to the ground, his voice rang out: "Hold, vermin, or die now!"

Islaen Connor's heart seemed to leap into her throat. The words were Arcturian, haughty, coldly triumphant, merciless, the command of an officer who had surrounded and surprised members of a surplanetary Resistance movement, and behind it was all the awesome authority of a war prince of the Arcturian Empire.

For one terrible, incredible instant, it was as if time had been thrown backward, and shock and stunned horror gripped everyone around her, Federation party and pirates alike.

The shade of doom seemed to clasp Geord of Hades in its bitter embrace, but he had not survived nearly a lifetime of savage guerrilla warfare because either his wits or his body responded slowly to sudden emergency. His homeworld had not been so long at peace that he had forgotten any of the hard lessons learned in the long years of hate and sudden death. Instinct and will beat back the crippling surprise shackling his limbs, and scarcely a moment passed before he was in command of himself once more.

He saw the shadowy figure on the tongue gather itself to drop to the ground, and he snapped the blaster already in his hand into position, discharging it on broad beam even as the invader made his leap.

Sogan jumped to the right, although he realized that he would have an easier time dealing with the spacer holding the other side. This Geord was probably the most dangerous of their opponents and almost certainly the one best able to rally and control his basically unruly party. It was imperative that he be taken out of operation as quickly as possible, before he could disrupt the attack or organize any kind of effective action against it.

The former Admiral did not underestimate this foe. Thorne had taught him the level of skill a Resistance fighter must have, and the little he had seen of this one was more than enough to instill a sharp respect for his abilities. Still, he had not expected either the speed of his recovery or the quickness of his response. Varn gasped and fell rather than sprang as the Hadesi's bolt burned across his right shoulder, lighting every nerve in his body with agony.

His weapon dropped uselessly to the ground, but Sogan kept his grip on consciousness and flung himself at his enemy even as he fell, striking against his legs and bringing him to the ground.

Geord's hold loosened on his blaster as he went down. It was only for a moment, but the Arcturian had been watching for it. He snatched it by the barrel and in the same motion swung with it, striking his opponent squarely in the face with its butt.

The renegade went down, blood spurting from his face as if he had been hit with an axe. He stayed down.

Sogan quickly slithered to the edge of the sheltering outcropping, willing himself to ignore the blistering pain in his shoulder. The others had apparently gotten through, and by the sound of it, a major battle was raging in the arsenal. He could not move far, handicapped as he was, but he had a fairly good view of the field from here, and could shoot well enough left-handed to make use of it.

Larnse Greggs watched the progress of the assault from his vantage at the lip of the crevice.

Sogan's initial attack had been successful, although he had not escaped it unscathed, and the Colonel, following fast after him, had dropped the second sentry from the outcropping and then another two of those still gathered beside the planetbuster. The rest had scattered and taken cover after that, and they were now exchanging heavy fire with the two off-worlders and with Jake Karmikel, who had joined the fray a few seconds before.

He could not say at this point what the outcome would be

or whether his own intervention would be required, but he thought it would go to the Federation unit.

They were good. He had to admit that. Wherever they had gotten their training and under whatever conditions it had been honed, he could scarcely imagine more expert close-quarter fighters than the two Noreenans.

Sogan was not doing badly either, despite his wound, which had rendered his right arm all but useless. The outcropping gave him good cover, but his opponents had that as well, and two of them were lying still, with the black path of a blaster bolt burned through the head of one and the heart of the second. Geord, of course, had been brought down in the first—

Greggs stiffened. The renegade was not dead. He moved, and even as Greggs watched, he lifted himself very slightly so that he could see what was going on around him.

His face was a mask of blood, but such injuries often appeared worse than they actually were. This seemed to be the case here, for he looked from Sogan's back to the abandoned blaster lying near him and quietly moved toward it.

Larnse Greggs glanced from one man to the other. The off-worlder, this one who looked and spoke Arcturian as if he were a member of that accursed race and who bore the mark of their hatred, was completely unaware of his peril, nor was he likely to become aware of it, not with the commotion of the battle and the mind-drugging pain of his wound to mask whatever sound the Hadesi might make. There would be no noise, no wasted or extravagant movement. Geord would make certain of that. He would not give Sogan a second opening against him.

Greggs' blaster discharged. It had been set to narrow beam at full strength, and its bolt tore downward like the wrath of a furious god, searing through the renegade's helmet and the skull beneath it as if they had no more substance than a cave spider's web.

Varn Tarl Sogan started to glance back at the sound of the death scream so close behind him, but the stench of florase gas and charring flesh caused him to whirl completely around.

What he saw drew all color from his face and would have unmanned him had an angry bolt sizzling close to his good shoulder not sharply recalled him to his own situation and forced him to take action in his own defense once more.

Still, he shuddered violently as he turned from the nearly headless corpse, and he prayed in his heart that the Hadesi, renegade though he was, had been dead, fully dead, before that chemical reaction had begun.

The battle raged on for another fifteen minutes, then abruptly it was over. The silence came so suddenly and completely that it seemed more unnatural and painful than the turmoil preceding it had been.

Jake's voice sounded over Sogan's communicator. "Come on out. We've cleared them."

The Arcturian got to his feet a little unsteadily. *Islaen?*

All life froze within him. There was no reply. Nothing . . .

Only for a moment did that deadly silence persist. *I'm here, Varn.*

Relief flooded him, but so, too, did a new surge of fear. The Commando radiated sharp pain with that response.

"Jake, she is hit!"

He started to race for the place her mind had pinpointed. Even as he did, he saw Islaen rise from behind the stalagmite that had served as her cover during the last phase of the fighting. She succeeded in gaining her feet but stood bent nearly in half, wavering and obviously incapable of moving out to meet him.

Varn reached her, put his sound arm around her to give her what support he could. *Islaen, how bad?*

"It's not much," she gasped, speaking aloud through tightly drawn lips, since Karmikel was now beside her as well. "Painful but not actually significant."

"We'll take care of it," the redhead assured her.

He glanced at the Arcturian. "I'll see to her, Admiral. You look nearly as badly off as she does. Just get the renewer out of her pack."

The Colonel, following Commando custom, had kept her gear with her, and Sogan was not long in locating it, working it open, and removing the healing device.

Jake had eased Islaen to the ground and ripped her tunic back to expose her wound by the time he returned to them.

Varn's eyes closed. He handed the ray to the other and knelt beside the wounded woman.

Liar! he hissed savagely.

Islaen looked up at him in surprise. Her lips parted as her eyes met his. Tears?

Her hand reached for his and quickly closed over it.

Easy. It's dirty and nasty-looking but not as bad as it seems, not with the renewer at hand. In truth.

Her face tightened as a spasm of pain tore through her. "Hurry up, Jake!—There's a lot of skin and muscle damage, but the organs are sound. I've run a check on myself. The faster you put that ray to work, the sooner you'll both be convinced I'm right."

Her eyes closed then, and a moment later she gave a sigh of relief as the effects of the renewer began to make themselves felt.

Varn brushed her hair back, stroking it gently. He had to use his injured arm since his sound hand still clasped hers, but he was conscious of no sensation of pain in himself. Only his consort's was real to him now, and that was ebbing fast.

At last she opened her eyes again and smiled up at him. He managed to return it, although the shadows of fear and grief were still strong within him. Without the intervention of the renewer, such a burn as she had sustained would have been extremely serious, and most probably fatal under almost any field conditions. It would have certainly been fatal in the face of the strenuous trek they must still make before they could return to the surface. He had instinctively reacted to that and to the intensity of the pain she had been radiating, but now the ray had worked its miracle, and he could see that her own assessment had been correct. The wound was closed, and already the newly generated skin was smooth and fair over it.

He helped Islaen to sit up when she indicated she wished to do so. She smiled at Karmikel and held out her hand to take the renewer from him.

"Thanks, friend. That feels a whole lot better." She gave a quick glance around their recent battlefield. "You'd better help Greggs check out those pirates, Jake. Some of them might be shamming. See if they're carrying anything that might be of interest to Intelligence. I'll take care of the Admiral's shoulder."

"Aye, Colonel."

The former Commando quickly put distance between himself and the pair, then his pace slowed and his head lowered.

He had known for a long time that Islaen Connor loved that man, and he knew she was happy in her marriage, but he had pitied her as well—aye, and prided himself in thinking that he might have given her more, been a better, more suitable match for her, had she chosen to accept his hand.

It had seemed impossible to him that Varn Tarl Sogan, once lord over a harem of his ultrasystem's most beautiful women, could return a fraction of what he received from her or at all appreciate the unique worth, the glory, of the Federation woman he had won. The cold formality of his usual manner with others served only to reinforce the belief that her lot with him was less than it could or should be. Even though Jake recognized it to be in a great part only a mask, a shield, it still seemed to declare that Sogan could give her little tenderness or real companionship.

These last few days had put the lie to all that. The way Varn had jumped Greggs after the assault on Islaen would have been enough in itself to prove him wrong, and just now . . . He had seen how the war prince had looked at her in that moment when they had both believed her to be dying, and later, while she was healing but still in pain. Whatever his own feelings were or had been for this woman who had been his commander and was still, apparently, fated to be his comrade, he knew now that they could not equal Sogan's. Even in that he was forced to step aside.

Varn looked uncertainly after the redhead. *Perhaps I should help them*— he began.

When I've fixed that shoulder. I don't want you passing out on me once the excitement's over and the reaction really sets in.—Here, sit on that crate over there so I can get at it properly.

The Arcturian obeyed. He had to confess to himself that it felt good to get off his feet again, although he had been standing only a few minutes.

Go ahead, Colonel, he told her and braced himself to hold steady while she carefully cut the charred cloth away from his wound.

The ray started its work almost as soon as she activated it. The sudden cessation of the worst of the pain proved nearly too much for him. He swayed and would have fallen forward had it not been for the quick support she gave.

Sorry, he muttered.

Gently, friend, Islaen said. *Sit still for a few minutes. As usual, you've been pushing yourself, and bodies do tend to protest that kind of mistreatment.*

She smiled. *Don't worry. This ray'll have you back to yourself in no time.*

TWENTY-SEVEN

SOGAN STRODE SWIFTLY across the floor of the arsenal toward the place where he had made his stand.

In truth, he wanted no part of examining what lay there. The glimpse he had had of it was enough, but he knew the others had not gotten to it yet, and he wanted to spare them the necessity of doing this.

He particularly wanted to shield Greggs. The Hadesi had begun on the left side of the tongue and was working his way around the chamber. It seemed to him to be a fairly obvious maneuver, and the only plea he could make under the circumstances, to avoid or at least postpone as long as possible contact with this corpse. It had, after all, been that of his sole remaining blood kin and the only other from his cell to survive the War.

Varn watched the guide for a moment without seeming to do so. Larnse was unguarded as he went about his grim task, and he looked to be what he in fact was—one utterly alone in the universe. It was an isolation the Arcturian exile knew too well himself, and he grieved for the man.

His eyes dropped again. Greggs had hated Geord and had wanted him dead, but he had loved him once, or so Sogan believed. It had taken strength to aim and fire that blaster, particularly for the sake of the one whose life he had thereby saved.

He knelt by the body. Trying not to look at what remained above the neck, he carefully went over it seeking papers or any other clue that might lead Federation authorities to some of the pirate starships or, better, reveal the whereabouts of the fleet itself.

It was not quick work, but at last he rose and started for the next corpses, those he had slain in the fighting. After that he would go on to the pair lying near the planetbuster, if Jake or Larnse had not reached them by then.

Bethe Danlo was near them, crouched before the big missile, but she had no time to devote to the dead. She did not seem to be aware of them at all.

Bandit was with her. Islaen had given the signal releasing them a few minutes before, when she felt reasonably sure none of their enemies would rise up to burn the demolitions expert as she emerged through the crevice. The gurry had streaked into the chamber, frantic with alarm for her two injured humans, but when she had assured herself that they were both all right, she returned to the spacer to watch her more interesting and less gruesome work.

Sogan had completed an unproductive search of the first pirate and was about to start on the other when he heard the sharp report of a discharging blaster.

His head snapped in the direction of the sound. Larnse Greggs. He was standing over one of the felled spacers.

Karmikel heard the sound as well. He was closer and saw more of what had occurred. "You bastard!" he roared as he flung himself toward the Hadesi, taking care not to make himself a target for a second shot.

The former Admiral raced for the pair and reached them moments after Jake had slammed into the guide.

Greggs was fighting to defend himself, but he had not attempted to use his weapon again, and he was withholding the more deadly blows he was capable of delivering.

Varn caught hold of the Noreenan and flung him back with a strength surprising in one of his build. Before the two men could join again, he sent a stream of blaster fire crackling between them, as Islaen had done to separate Greggs and him in the spaceport office.

As on that first occasion, the antagonists froze. Neither appeared inclined to continue the attack, but the Arcturian did not lower his weapon as he looked from one to the other.

"You first, Karmikel," he commanded.

"That man was still alive," the former Commando spat. "This misbegotten cur executed him."

Islaen Connor had reached them by then. Her blaster was in her hand as well, so Sogan holstered his and knelt beside the body.

The death-bolt had been set very narrow and had burned directly through the center of the forehead. It had been delivered within the past several minutes.

With his knife he tore the saturated cloth away from an older wound in the breast. The man had taken the full force of a wide beam. The seared area seemed vast in the broad chest. Bleeding had been heavy, and there was still sign of bubbling in the congealing liquid.

He stood again. "Burned through the lungs. He would not have survived."

"The renewer—" Jake began.

"It cannot repair organ damage, as you are well aware. At best it would have delayed the inevitable, but we could not have brought him back with us. By the time we had returned for him, he would have been dead, from the cold if nothing else."

"We might have attempted to save him all the same."

Larnse Greggs gave a bitter laugh. "Leave an inevitably dying man down here, maybe to awake to find himself utterly alone, with the dark and cold ravening for him just beyond the little circle of his lamplight, with no other creature near save the waiting cave beetles and no sound unless it be his own screams? I wouldn't do that to an Arcturian!" He eyed the readhead contemptuously. "Don't try to tell me you Commandos never had to kill a wounded man, comrades of your own."

"In need," he hissed. "Only in direst need! That wasn't the case here."

The Colonel raised her hand for silence. "Let it rest, Jake. As Varnt said, the man was dying. I would've done it your way, put him out with as strong a sedative as we dared use and striven against hope to save him, but Greggs may have made the kinder choice. We'll just have to leave it at that."

She looked down at the corpse and then back at her comrades. "You and Varnt finish the examination. There are only a couple of bodies left anyway."

Islaen started to turn away, trying with only partial success to conceal her own anger and disgust. Her readings told her that the Hadesi's motives had been genuine, but there was too much unavoidable violence in her life for her to stomach needless slaughter.

She felt Sogan's thought reach out to hers; tentatively, as always when he felt uncertain of his reception.

Aye, friend?

I should have tried to spare him as well.

I know that, as does Jake.

A shudder passed through her mind, although she succeeded in keeping it from becoming visible.

I wish we were well out of this. I don't think I'll feel clean again until we're back in space, with Hades of Persephone no more than an ugly memory.

Both of them froze almost in the same instant, the Commando in response to the wave of fear suddenly ripping into her receptors, Varn because of its echo from Bandit.

"Bethe!" she exclaimed aloud, to alert the other two men as she raced toward the demolitions expert.

Sogan followed her. *Bandit, what is wrong?*

Bethe scared. Hurry, Varn, Islaen! Fix!

The off-worlders reached the planetbuster, and then there was no need to ask the cause of the spacer's fear. There was a steady, low, but distinctly perceptible hum emanating from it. The missile was active.

"When did it start?" Sogan demanded.

Bethe glanced up at him, then back at the deadly thing before her. "I don't know. It was going when I got the plate off. I couldn't hear it before that.—I'll have to try to pull the rods."

"How long do we have?" asked Karmikel, who had just come up behind her in company with Larnse Greggs.

"I don't know that, either. It depends on how long it's been going and what time and moisture have done to its innards.—You might try making a run for it up the tunnels."

"What's the point?" the Noreenan asked grimly. "Nothing in this area, aboveground or below, will survive if it explodes. If we're about to go to our respective afterworlds, we might as well disembark together."

He squatted down beside her. "Come on, Sogan. Let's see

what we can do to help the Sergeant. You're about the best I've ever seen with machines.''

Not with Federation weaponry, he thought grimly, but he knelt on the other side of Bethe from Jake.

"What would you have us do?" he asked.

She started to reply that she could make no use of their offer, but stopped herself. "You just may be able to help," she said instead. "There are extra female wrenches in my kit. Take one of them, each of you. C-size."

She pointed to the newly exposed interior of the planetbuster. "See, there are the rods I told you about. Each of them is held in place by two retaining pins, these things right here, both of which must be loosened sufficiently for me to draw the rod out. I've gotten the bolts off, but the pins themselves are plaguey stiff. Try to turn them until they're loose enough to pull back a little, but by all this wretched planet's gods, don't jerk them or lose your grip and slam those wrenches around in there, or we're all done."

Varn Tarl Sogan nodded his understanding, although she did not look up to see it. He quickly located a wrench and cautiously slid it over the pin, slowly tightening it when he felt the head come in contact with the roof of the socket.

He grimaced as he began to apply careful, steady pressure. Bethe had been right in stating the thing was stiff, and he felt a moment's helpless fear. If it were so badly seized that it required lube or cutting oils to free it, they were lost. They would never be given that much time.

It came loose, not in a dramatic jerk, but in a fraction turn followed by another nearly as hard-won.

"I have it. What about you, Jake?"

"It's coming.—Bethe, what next?"

"When I tell you, pull them out as far as you can. I'll try the rod."

She raised her own larger wrench. "All right. Start now."

Slowly, agonizingly slowly, the pins moved outward, but every gain was won only after a fight with the forces that had built up to freeze them in place over the long decades of disuse, and neither off-worlder knew if he would be able to bring his out far enough to free the rod without a fatal application of violence or an equally fatal delay. There could be only seconds left to them now. . . .

Bethe Danlo knew that as well, but she gave no sign of the fear that was on her or of the awesome burden of responsibility she bore. Her small hands were rock steady as they guided the wrench over its target and then ever so slowly tightened it. She began to pull, stopped.

"A little more," she whispered to her aides.

Once again she began to draw it forth. This time her breath froze, consciously, so that her body should not be rocked by even that gentle natural process.

The rod came to her. With infinite patience and an iron control of will that compelled her to keep her movements slow and deliberate, she continued to pull it toward her.

The humming ceased, and Bethe rocked back on her heels, her eyes closed, the rod free in the air before her, held only by the wrench in her tightly clenched hands.

Not even for a single moment did she remain in that position.

"Now for the other one. It could start up again if we don't get it out quickly."

Once more the demolitions expert went through the careful, tense process, but in the end she sat with the two rods lying together across her lap, smiling up at her comrades.

"We've done it," she told them, triumph and relief clear in her voice and in her face. "That planetbuster's nothing more than so much junk now. It won't threaten anyone again."

TWENTY-EIGHT

BETHE DANLO DARTED up the ladder of the *Jovian Moon*. She found Jake in the surprisingly large crew's cabin with a maze of diagrams and papers, chiefly lists of various kinds, spread out on the table before him.

He raised his hand in greeting. "Welcome, Bethe! Come and look. I'm revamping my plans for the *Moon*."

Her eyes sparkled. "She's a fine ship as she is, and I thought your plans were excellent as they were."

"Well, they've just been upgraded, and the timetable's been fast-forwarded." He grinned. "The Navy's going to be picking up the tab."

Her bright smile answered his. "You have reenlisted, then!"

"Aye," he confessed. "Admiral Sithe made me an offer I couldn't refuse, even apart from the work on my ship. I've got my old rank back, and I haven't even lost seniority time." He scowled. "He said he figured I'd eventually come to my senses and had me listed as being on extended leave instead of demobilized. I'm actually to collect back pay. He said since I'd been doing Commando work anyway, I might as well draw salary for it."

"I know, but I wasn't so sure you wouldn't be too stubborn to jump at it once the offer was made."

The Noreenan gave her a sharp look. "What do you mean, you know?"

"The Admiral told me, of course."

"Oh.—Well, it seems Ram Sithe's decided to use Islaen and Sogan as a special troubleshooting team. They've proven they can work so well together and get such excellent results

192

under crisis conditions that he wants to put them at it permanently, and he wants me with them. Since I seem fated for that, I agreed.''

His features shadowed. "I was leery about accepting my commission again," he confessed. "I'd resigned it originally because I couldn't stand bearing the weight of worlds on my shoulders—"

He stopped. He did not know why he was telling her this but realized he wanted her to know, and so, more hesitantly, he went on.

"Sithe said he'd reviewed my tests carefully and believed that the break I've had was enough to restore me, and I feel that I'm ready to take it all on again. I went through a battery of new tests, needless to say, and they all confirm that. Sithe did promise that if it doesn't work, if I find that I do want out, I can have it, no questions, no shame, and no trouble."

He spread his hands. "So here I am, Commando-Captain Jake Karmikel once more."

"You have my full congratulations, my friend."

The newly restored Commando studied her speculatively. It was in character for Ram Sithe to personally interview and thank one who had performed as Bethe Danlo had on Hades of Persephone, but he would not have casually discussed Commando business, or his plans for any individual Commando, with an outsider, and a civilian to boot.

"I think you have a story of your own, Bethe Danlo."

Once more her eyes danced, sending glimmers of silver through their usually cool slate. "It's Sergeant Bethe Danlo. He got me too. I wasn't favored with that extended leave business, and certainly got no back pay, but I start out with my old rank, and my full service time and credit come with me. That's what took me so long getting back here even though he saw me before he did you. I had to go through all the reenlistment and adjustment proceedings."

"Why, Bethe?"

"Why him or why me?"

"Both."

"Admiral Sithe thinks I have skills you three can use and appears satisfied that I can work with you."

There was a question in that, and Jake nodded. "You can,

and I can't think of anyone I'd welcome more," he assured her quietly, "but why did you let yourself in for it?"

The demolitions expert shrugged. "I suppose I wanted real work again, work directly important to people. I won't have to be defusing missiles as steady fare. That's not Commando business, and it's with you that I'll be serving.

"There are other benefits as well, of course. The pay's better than anything I can get on my own, and I'll be spending less on my keep and gear. That means more can go to the building of the future Danlo fleet."

She sighed. "I'll have to give up my present berth, naturally, since I can't be gadding around the ultrasystem when I might be needed on pretty short notice, but I suppose that's a small price to pay. Places should be easier to find if I decide to come out again after this hitch. The demobilization'll be well over by then and the glut on the market just about absorbed."

"You might find another berth now," he suggested tentatively.

Bethe shook her head. "Sogan won't go for that, not yet, anyway. He isn't ready for more company."

"I didn't mean on the *Maid*," Karmikel replied steadily.

Bethe colored as the memory of some of the things she had said to him in Hades' underworld returned. "I'm not asking any favors, Jake Karmikel!"

"And I'm not offering any!—This ship's big for one man. I can manage her by myself and had resigned myself to the fact that I'd have to since I can't afford to hire anyone at this stage and wouldn't dare bring in an outsider anyway now that I'm back with the Commandos again, but the truth of the matter is that I do need help. You'd be ideal. The Navy's paying you, we've proven we can work together, and I like your style, in space and on-world. Don't think I haven't watched how you've handled yourself."

He, too, recalled their conversation on Hades. "I'm not looking to take on any charters, either. You don't have to worry your head about that."

"No fear of it!" She quelled the illogically sharp surge of annoyance and smiled. "Come, Captain. It seems you'd be getting all the benefit out of that arrangement."

"Not really. Your quarters'd be better than a barracks slot, for one thing, and you'd be just about your own boss here. The work'll be light. We'll mostly be testing new equipment and the like, that or flying on actual missions. You'd have to be present for both anyway. There won't be cargo or heavy stuff to contend with unless it's part of some assignment.''

He drummed his fingers on the paper-littered table. ''I won't promise what I might not fulfill, but if this does work out, I'd consider a partnership. I know that's not the same as mastering your own ship, but we'd both collect if we left the service and took up private business again, and you could eventually sell your share back to me when you're ready to go your own way.—What do you say, Bethe? Would you like time to think on it?''

The demolitions expert shook her head. ''None whatsoever,'' she answered, smiling broadly. ''I wouldn't be my father's daughter if I passed up a potential chance to gain a half share in a starship as fine as this one.''

She held out her hand to him. ''Captain Karmikel, you have just acquired a crew for the *Jovian Moon*.''

Islaen Connor paused just inside the *Maid*'s hatch. *Varn? I am on the bridge, Islaen.*

The former Admiral had been stretched out on his pilot's seat reading, but quickly rose to his feet when he saw her.

She greeted him cheerfully, but her eyes shadowed momentarily when they fell on the report of their mission to Hades. This was not the first time she had seen him with it since they had set their seals on it, and he always seemed more down, even more withdrawn, when he had finished with it.

Something was lashing him hard, but she could only guess at what it was. Sogan had shut himself behind shields tighter than she had ever before known in him since they had lifted from that thrice-accursed planet. He scarcely permitted enough contact between them to allow conversation, and sometimes that only an a verbal level.

At first she had been annoyed, then angry, but by now she was chiefly worried. He appeared worn out. If he did not work this through very soon, she would have to try to force matters, whatever the consequences. For now, though, for a little while longer, she would continue to go along with him.

Islaen set the safe-lock portfolio she was carrying down on the instrument panel without commenting on the report and sat on the arm of her own flight chair. Her hands automatically curved to receive and cuddle Bandit, who flew to her from Varn's shoulder.

I'm glad that's over! she exclaimed with genuine relief. *Ram Sithe can drag more out of a person during a debriefing than anyone else I've ever met.*

To her surprise, Varn smiled. *That is one mark of a brilliant commander, Colonel.*

His dark eyes fell to the report, but he soon raised them again. *I am glad it is over as well, all of it.*

Once more he looked down, but this time he did not face her again as quickly. *I have been thinking about them, Greggs and his compatriots.*

He could not, or rather, did not try, to keep his distaste from his voice.

There is no denying their courage, their strength of will, their devotion to what they hold to be right, yet . . .

He shook his head. *I must be grateful I did not encounter them during the War. I have always prided myself that I never commanded in the manner of an Orlan Fran Uskorn or his son after him, but I would not have responded to those people as I did to the Thornens. Had I been set over them, perhaps I might in the end have fought my war even as the Uskorns did.*

His fingers brushed the cover of the report. *We warped them, I suppose, made them that they are.*

No. You did not.

Her reply came so swiftly and with such certainty that he looked at her in some amazement, but Islaen continued somberly before he could question her.

I've been thinking about this too. Plenty. The Hadesim are what they always were. The pressures put on them by the invasion and occupation were admittedly extreme, but they acted as a crucible, refining what was already present. The offspring of Hades were altered. Of course they were, but it was in accordance with their own nature. Thornens would have responded to the same circumstances differently, Noreenans differently still, and maybe they wouldn't have come out of it all nearly as well—or so much as survived it. You Arcturians were catalysts, my friend, but you were never gods. You might have had the power to destroy a race, but to remake its soul was quite beyond any of you.

You may be right, he said slowly after a silence of several seconds.

Maybe I am, maybe not, but I rather think I'm not too far off.

There was more. She could sense it, but she felt him draw back once again.

Varn Tarl Sogan forcibly turned his eyes from the report. That part of it could and must now be put to rest. He could not dwell in past violence or allow himself to wallow in guilt he had not even earned. It was with the knowledge Hades had awakened in him that he must deal, face up to the decision forced on him, but even that could be delayed for a little while yet.

He sat back himself and watched his consort curiously. A light had come into her eyes, and he could read the excitement on her.

You were a long time, he ventured, *even for one of Ram Sithe's debriefings.*

Oh, we had more to talk about than that! He has plans for us.

Such as?

Actually, it's more a paper upgrade to get us the official status and appropriate benefits than anything else, since we've been doing the work all along. He wants to make us a special, autonomous unit operating directly under him to handle some of the real crises that keep cropping up, those involving major populations, large-scale pirate activity, and the like.

Sogan smiled, rejoicing in her pride. *The elite of the elite,* he remarked. *Congratulations, Colonel, although it is but just recognition of your abilities.*

Our abilities, she corrected him a little sharply, *and it's not just us, either. Jake's on the job again and will be serving with us.*

He chuckled. *That comes as no surprise. I had been expecting to see him back in uniform before now. If ever a man belonged in our work, Jake Karmikel does.*

Bethe Danlo will likely pair with him. . . .

Bethe? he asked in surprise.

She nodded. *Aye. Admiral Sithe liked our report of the way she managed herself on Hades, and dropped a net over her too. It was quick work, but I've never known him to misjudge anyone.*

He made no mistake with her, Varn agreed.

Islaen glanced down in response to a delighted whistle from the gurry still nestled in her hand. "I know you're pleased, love. She was one of your conquests from the start."

Sogan laughed. *I suppose her vote settles it.*

Naturally!

The Colonel grew serious once more. *You do like her, don't you, Varn?*

Bethe? Aye, very much. I would trust my instinct and take her on even without access to the information your Admiral Sithe has in her files.

Varn Tarl Sogan stopped speaking suddenly. He realized all too clearly what he was saying, what he was doing, and he smothered the excitement rippling within him. It was sooner than he had expected—or permitted himself to expect—but the time had come to stop acting the coward. This must go no further if he were to have no part in it.

"Islaen?"

Something in her heart froze. Here it was. The note she heard in the former Admiral's voice struck her as would the sound of her own death knell. Or his.

She compelled herself to answer him quietly, as if she anticipated no more than a continuation of the discussion he had so abruptly terminated.

"Aye?" she asked, switching into the audible speech he had chosen.

For an instant Sogan thought his courage would fail him, but he faced her squarely and went on.

"Do you wish to be released from this union?"

"No, I don't!" Islaen snapped, surprise making her answer more frank in phrase and tone than it otherwise might have been.

Her fingers uncurled from around the gurry. "Leave us, Bandit. This must be settled between we two alone."

The little creature looked alarmed and radiated alarm, but she took wing at once without uttering a sound and streaked off the bridge.

Once she had gone, Islaen Connor fixed her consort with flashing eyes. "Let's have it, Varn, and make sure it's the truth. If you want out of this, say it, but take the responsibility yourself. Don't be throwing it over on me. I'll do a lot for you, but I won't be your scapegoat."

"It is not a matter of wanting," he said desperately, then forced himself to speak more calmly. "I love you, and I realize that you love me, but the fact remains that our marriage was a mistake for you. I cannot see you bound forever in it."

She frowned. "Mistake? You've said that before.—Varn, if you're still dwelling on what happened on Hades, I'm going to be more furious than I am right now. All right. You were wrong to go in the first place, and you might've wrecked everything if you'd killed Greggs, but those were hardly the first serious mistakes you've made in your life, and they sure as all space won't be the last."

The Noreenan glared at him. "I blew up at you because I'd fallen into your own habit of expecting the superhuman from you. That part of it was my problem, not yours."

He shook his head in despair. Why was she making this so difficult for him?

"Federation and Empire are different, Islaen Connor. I have come to see that more and more clearly during our time together. I am not a man of your ultrasystem. Your ways are not mine, and I cannot be to you the consort you have a right to expect. Your husband should at least be able to share your life with you."

He seemed to be staring into some dark void.

"Do you remember when we were watching those little things swimming in that cave pool? Islaen, I could not even bring myself to go down beside you to enjoy them with you."

"You enjoyed them all the same, and enjoyed my pleasure in them as well."

The ghost of a smile softened his features for an instant before dying again.

"My delight has always been in yours."

He came to his feet suddenly and turned from her. "That is not enough. Not for you."

Her head snapped up. "By whose judgment? Do you think I was some little fool led blindly into a relationship whose consequences I didn't understand at all? I knew you damn well, Varn Tarl Sogan, and I knew precisely what I was getting.—Have the grace to look at me at least, since you're trying to fling me out of your life!''

Sogan whirled around, stung. "Not that!"

"Then listen to me, and listen good. I not only married the man I wanted, but the kind of man as well. I only loved once before you, but you can take my word for it that Morris Martin was so much like you in some ways that the resemblance is frightening.''

Her temper cooled. She knew she had at least a hold on him now and pressed her advantage more quietly.

"Do you think I mind that you internalize your pleasures more than most do or that we share them in a more intimate fashion? Varn, in truth, you're not the same with me as you are with others, but even were that not so, the talent we both have would still take me to the man behind that mask you wear. It does now. I know that you share my life, share it fully, and when you permit it, I know, I can experience, something of the depth of your feeling for me. No other woman has so much. Why should you imagine I need more?''

She took a deep breath. "I'm going to drop my shields. Completely. Read me. See if there's any shade of doubt or regret in me.''

The Arcturian stepped back. "That would violate—"

"Do it. If you do not, this will always be there to gnaw at you. We face too many real problems without making our own.''

Still he held back, and once more her eyes flashed.

"This is the Federation, Admiral Sogan. The accused have a right to trial here. You have cast question on the soundness of my choice and, therefore, on my ability to choose. My own mind is my expert witness, and I demand that it be called and its testimony be heard.''

For a long while he made no move at all, until she was certain she had lost. Then she felt his mind come to hers.

Varn's approach was hesitant, filled with embarrassment and shame that he should be so invading her innermost being. Relief followed quickly as he learned what he wanted desperately to know and had convinced himself he could never hope to find.

Tenderness flooded her, and happiness such as she had never imagined this man could feel.

She was conscious of a nameless struggle within him. All at once it ended. His own inner shields went down, and the war prince offered to her the same incredible confidence she had just given to him.

It all came to her, the decision that had damned him, the shame and infinite grief of defeat and the horror that had followed so fast upon it, the years of fear which had been a living death to him, the wonder and joy in renewed life, and now . . . Could any woman be worthy of this?

Varn Tarl Sogan laughed almost fiercely, reading and answering her question in the same instant. All life and all the future were before him, and he looked to them both with an excitement and eagerness he had not allowed to himself since that fateful moment when he had given Thorne her life and shattered his own.

Islaen felt and shared the triumph and new hope waking so suddenly within him, and when he opened his arms to her, she came gladly to him, glorying in the strength and gentleness of his embrace and in the marvel of the bond uniting them.

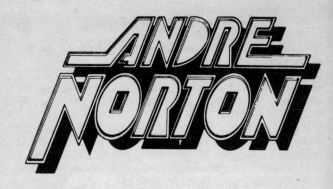

THE WITCH WORLD SERIES